ONE LITTLE PUSH

Kate Leonard

For Louise, my oldest friend

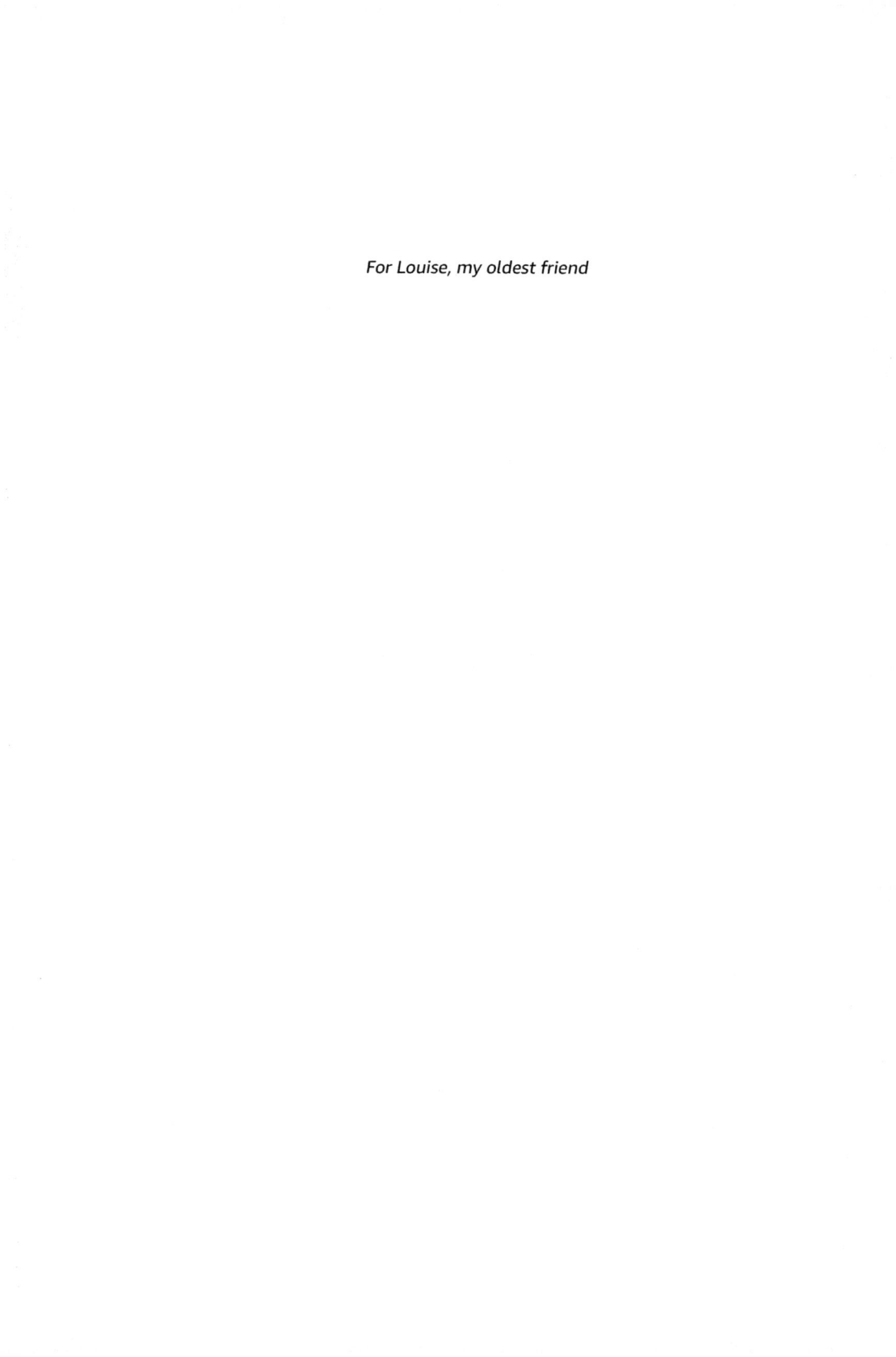

CONTENTS

Title Page	1
Dedication	3
Prologue	7
PART ONE	10
PART TWO	124
Acknowledgement	215
About The Author	217
Books By This Author	219
Afterword	223

PROLOGUE

It's an awe-inspiring sight. Malham Cove, one of Yorkshire's most dramatic landmarks. A towering wall of rock, rising over eighty metres up into the sky. The huge cliff face forms an uncannily perfect curve, made, they say, by the thunderous waterfall that existed here over twelve thousand years ago. The rock is stark white, streaked with grey, but here and there stunted pines and meagre shrubs cling on desperately to small ledges, giving a sudden flash of green.

On a calm summer day, the valley is benign. The beck flows prettily from a cave at the foot of the cliff and tourists gawp and take selfies. Hikers chat. Picnics are unwrapped and children play.

But on a dark day when the sky becomes stormy, the Cove is a dangerous place. The weather can turn in an instant and the rocks become slippery, treacherous. The four hundred-odd stone steps that lead up to the top of the Cove must be treated with respect. It's a long way down.

Upon reaching the top, the full, mad splendour of the Cove is revealed. A vast expanse of flat, grey rock stretches before you, broken up into odd, lumpy squares by deep cracks and crevices. It resembles nothing so much as row upon row of rotting molars, thrusting up from the surface. It is bare, desolate, unforgiving. Another world. Nothing much grows here. Easy to slip and fall into the cracks, breaking an ankle. Tempting, also, to approach the edge of the cliff and peer down over the valley, hundreds of feet below. There is no barrier. Nothing to break a fall. The clouds draw in around you and it can be so easy to lose your sense of direction.

Geologists long ago explained this landscape to students. The acid in rainwater reacts with the calcium of the limestone rock, eroding it, seeking out little cracks or weaknesses, and slowly, slowly widening and deepening them into grooves. Over time, you are left with a pavement of rocky slabs called clints, and deep fissures called grikes.

Rainwater and time, so simple, causing such destruction. Eroding, exposing, eating away, insidious and relentless.

People do the same thing. Some people.

All those little insults, the casual sarcasm, the mockery, just like the rainwater, drip, drip, dripping onto the victim, seeking out the cracks in the armour of self-esteem. Once the fault lines are discovered, the fun starts. The verbal blows are well aimed now, forcing the cracks wider and deeper, letting the acid seep in, until the unlucky victim is exposed, naked and defenceless as a new-born.

Some might call it bullying, but it's more than that. Bullying is too soft a term. It is the systematic destruction of character. The peeling away, layer by layer, of the person you are trying to become.

It can lead to suicide.

But it can also lead to murder.

At the foot of the great cliff lies a dark, twisted shape. It is barely discernible behind the jumble of fallen rock and the gnarled old tree, bent double by the wind. On closer inspection you notice a little flash of colour; the blue is surely too vibrant to be a natural material. Has a careless hiker left their jacket behind? Or their backpack? Closer still and you see an arm, splayed out at an unnatural angle, and your heart beats faster. A body! Oh God, please, don't let it be... But suddenly there's movement - yes! Surely the person is alive! You run the last few paces.

And stop dead. A pair of crows are disturbed and lift away from the head, cawing angrily.

The soft meat of the eyeballs has been pecked clean to reach the brain tissue within, leaving two empty sockets.

Malham Cove has claimed another victim.

PART ONE

Chapter One

Now

Erin opened the passenger door wide and perched sideways on the seat to lace up her old walking boots. Then she straightened up and scanned the road above where it zig-zagged across the hillside. She thought she caught a flash of bright blue between the high hedgerows. Thank God! That peacock blue! That had to be Laura's car. Laura would be able to lift her spirits, give her some good, sensible advice and put her back on the right track. She'd been feeling jumpy, bitter and confused for weeks now. Laura would sort her out.

She grabbed the backpack from the back seat and felt inside the pocket. Yes, her phone was there. Water bottle, waterproof, sun cream – that was a bit optimistic, given the typical Yorkshire weather today. Slate-grey clouds hung low over the fields, and rain threatened. It wasn't the best day for a walk, but she'd spent the morning fizzing with pent-up frustration. She knew if she hadn't got out of the house there was a danger she would have exploded. Said things she'd later regret.

She checked the instructions that she'd found on the internet and printed out earlier that day. A six-mile walk around the village of Emley. It didn't look too difficult. The map was rather vague though, and her printer had run out of coloured ink, making the footpath an indistinct grey dotted line. Apparently the trick was to keep the enormous television mast constantly in sight to avoid getting lost. She gave a little snort of derision as she noticed the description: 'Yorkshire's own Eiffel Tower'. A bit of an exaggeration, she thought, turning to regard the mast. But it was rather beautiful: a slender tower of concrete sitting atop a sweep of rough moorland, three hundred and thirty metres tall, and tapering to an elegant point that did, in fact, give it a touch of Parisian chic.

She looked round as she heard a car approaching. Yes, that was Laura's blue Fiesta. She felt a wave of relief as her oldest friend pulled into the gravelled parking space.

'Hey,' she called, walking over to join her. 'Thank you so, so much for coming out today. You're an absolute angel. Did I stop you doing anything important?'

'No, not really. I was just doing a few odd jobs in the house. Nathan's at football practice and Richard's pottering about in the garden. It's good you called. And Dudley could do with a proper walk. He's getting a bit too fat.' Laura opened the hatchback and an aging cocker spaniel navigated the jump to the ground with obvious reluctance. 'What's this walk you've found, then?'

'Here, have a look.'

Erin showed her the photocopied pages and they read the first paragraph together, turning the map round and figuring out the starting point. Laura snapped the lead onto the dog's collar and they set off down the road, then branched off onto a narrow track that ran between a wooden fence and a dry stone wall. They walked in single file, passing a football field and pausing for a moment to watch a noisy group of young boys practicing penalty kicks. Laura bent down to unclip the lead and the old dog ran gamely ahead on stiff legs, sniffing at the grasses at the base of the stone wall and occasionally lifting a hind leg to leave his own mark.

The path skirted a housing estate, then broadened out as it crossed a sloping field, allowing them to walk two-abreast at last. Laura glanced over at Erin, taking in her tired eyes and anxious expression. She'd been friends with this woman since kindergarten and her role as loyal second had barely changed in all those years. Erin was the instigator, the one with the ideas. She'd been the naughty one in primary school, getting them both into trouble on several occasions. Laura still felt a stab of guilt when she remembered how they'd stolen their classmates' school trip money, which had been sitting unguarded on a low windowsill in the classroom. That had been Erin's idea, of course. 'Everyone's got those new trainers except us,' she'd said. 'That's not fair. If we take that money we can buy ourselves trainers too.' Laura had happily gone along with this logic, but when the crime had been discovered, it was Laura who immediately broke down and confessed. Erin had been unrepentant. There was a wild streak in Erin. Most of the time it lay hidden, but now and again it exploded with unexpected force. She was the more emotional of the two, her moods see-sawing up and down wildly. Over the years, Laura's job had been to temper and soothe, to dampen Erin's more dangerous impulses and calm her dark rages. But just sometimes, and more and more frequently these days, she felt heartily fed up with this role, although she rarely showed it.

'So what's up?' she asked now. 'I get the impression there's something you need to talk about.'

Erin let out a long sigh, shrugged and shook her head. 'I don't really know. I feel... I just feel like I'm going to scream all the time. I'm so wound up. Everything is irritating me. I've got this... sort of electricity inside me that won't go away.'

'Oh, OK. Give me an example. What irritates you?'

'Ted's driving me mad! Sometimes I can't even look at him.'

'Why? What's he done?'

'That's just it, he's done nothing. He does nothing! He sits in his armchair all weekend with his slippers on and watches TV. He shuffles about like an old grandad. He never wants to go anywhere or do anything new.'

'Oh, come on! Ted's a sweetie! He's solid and understanding and loyal. You're being too hard on him.'

'I know I am. But I can't help it. I keep snapping at him.'

'Well you know what I think about Ted. He's perfect for you. He balances you out. He's the calm to your crazy.'

'But I feel like he's sliding into old age already. No, not sliding; he's welcoming it in with open arms! I told him I was bored and wanted to go somewhere this weekend and he suggested the garden centre. The fucking garden centre! As if the most exciting thing he could think of was strolling round some plants and having a cup of tea in the café.'

'Well, what did you want to do?'

'I don't know. Something new. Different. I don't even know what.'

'OK, Erin, listen. I think I know what's wrong with you. You're blaming Ted for something that's not his fault. You're forty-nine years old. We both are. We both have this big birthday looming. Fifty. It feels like we've reached a kind of mid-point where everything will start to go downhill. You're just scared of getting old.'

'Yeah, maybe. But why should I give in to old age? Why shouldn't I grab the chances now to have some fun before it's too late?'

'What kind of fun are you talking about?' Laura frowned in disapproval. 'You're not thinking of having an affair, are you?'

Erin pulled a face. 'No, no, nothing like that. At least… chance would be a fine thing! No, I just want to live a bit. Experience things. Feel more intense emotions. I don't want to settle for this kind of half-life.'

'Have you told Ted how you feel?'

'I've tried. He doesn't understand. He just looks mystified and upset. He thinks it's because the kids have left home. Empty nest syndrome.'

'Yeah, well, there's some truth in that too, I expect. We all live a bit vicariously through our kids, and they give our days so much focus. Sorting out their crises, celebrating their successes. Your two have both left home now and you must feel a void. It will take time to adjust to that. That's normal.'

'Yeah, maybe you're right. I wish we'd had three kids, like you and Richard. Then we'd still have one at home. I envy you!'

'Well, yeah, but that's just pushing back the problem. It'll be the same for me in three years when Nathan finally goes to university – if he ever gets there. The way things are going now, I'm not at all sure... But look, it's too easy to blame Ted for how you're feeling. You need to sort yourself out. What about a new hobby? Art class? Choir? Tai chi?'

'Oh, come on! That all sounds terribly middle-class - and middle-aged too.'

'Face it, Erin - we are middle-aged.'

'No we're not. I refuse to be!'

Laura shook her head, exasperated. 'Oh, I don't know then... learn to parachute? Sky-dive?'

Erin laughed. 'Yeah, maybe I will!'

They reached a stile and watched the old dog trying and failing to find a way under it. Laura picked him up bodily and lifted him over, and they continued down a gentle incline towards a brook.

'What about work? How's that going?' asked Laura. 'Is that part of the problem?'

'No, not really. It's going OK. I like teaching the new Diploma in Travel and Tourism. This year's bunch of students are pretty motivated. It's quite relaxed and fun. No, work's not the problem. Anyway, enough about me. I'm fine really. I just needed to let off some steam. How are you? What's your news?'

About time, thought Laura, smiling inwardly. 'Oh, I'm fine. You know me. Too busy to worry about getting old or having fun. I'm just trying to survive. I wish I had the time to feel bored.'

Erin did feel a bit sheepish at this. Laura was a paediatric nurse, working long shifts and dealing with a constantly changing timetable. The emotional and physical demands were enormous, and Erin had no idea how Laura coped with infant deaths, childhood leukaemia, grieving parents, young victims of road accidents. It was a job she could never do herself, but Laura rarely complained.

'I'm sorry. You've got so much on your plate and I'm wittering on about nothing. You must think I'm a real whinger.'

'Well, yes, I do, rather,' Laura said. Erin shot her a look; this sounded like criticism, and was not what she expected from her friend. 'You've got a husband who adores you, a job you enjoy, two well-adjusted kids, no real money problems, and you're still not happy. You're a bit spoilt. You've got what most people can only dream about.'

The 'spoilt' stung a bit, but Erin knew it was probably deserved. 'I know! I know I'm being unreasonable,' she admitted. 'I try to give myself a lecture, but this kind of anger keeps bubbling up inside me. I can't help it.' She glanced over at Laura, taking in the dark shadows under her eyes. Her oldest friend was tall and slender with an almost boyish figure. Her shoulder-length auburn hair, which had always been her crowning glory, was showing streaks of grey and needed a good cut. 'I think we both need some more fun in our lives, but for different reasons. You work way too hard and you never put yourself first.'

The conversation petered out as the path grew steeper, forcing them to conserve their breath. At the top of the hill they paused by a dry stone wall, and looked down at the view. A shaft of sunlight broke through the clouds and played briefly over the fields, painting them an intense emerald green. Above them, the tip of the TV mast sparkled a pure white against the dark grey sky. It was a beautiful sight. Erin reached into her backpack for the bottle of water and packet of biscuits.

'Let's have a break. Here, have a digestive.' She offered the pack to Laura, who took two. 'You know, the first time we came up this way was with the youth club. Do you remember?'

'Yeah,' said Laura, warily. 'I remember. When we were sixteen.'

'I've been thinking about the old days a lot recently.'

'Have you?' A worried frown creased Laura's face. 'I'm not sure that's a good idea. You don't want to stir all that up again.'

'Hmm. You know, I joined the youth club because I was bored. I wanted more out of life. I had that same feeling that time was passing and I wasn't making the most of it. Like the way I'm feeling now.'

'Yeah, and look where that got us. It was a mistake. We both suffered a lot that year.'

'Oh, I'm not sure it was all a mistake. It was exciting. We were really living in the moment.'

'Right up until the accident. Have you forgotten that? Then it was hell.'

'Hmm,' replied Erin with a far-away look in her eyes. 'Are you still in contact with anyone from those days?'

'Not really. I used to get the odd Christmas card from Karen for a while, but nothing for years now. Why? Don't go stirring all that up again. It's not the solution, it's best to forget all about it.'

'I wonder what they're all doing now. Karen, Millie, the boys…'

'Stop it, Erin. You're looking back through rose-tinted glasses. It took me a long time and an awful lot of therapy to get over that year. Christ, don't you remember? The panic when we realised? Calling out the mountain rescue? The wait? Then having to identify the body? Oh, God, I can still see that body. Then all those endless police interviews? The enquiry? That unbearable funeral? Jesus, it was bloody horrendous! Just leave it alone. Go and find a… I don't know.. a historical enactment club or something to join, but don't go looking for answers to your current problems in the past. That year was the worst year of our lives. Leave it alone.'

'Yeah, you're right, as usual,' smiled Erin, but she didn't quite meet Laura's eye as she spoke.

'Promise?' pressed Laura.

'OK,' said Erin breezily. 'Come on. Let's get going again before the rain starts to fall.'

***

Erin drove home thinking about what Laura had said. She recognised the truth of her friend's words. Yes, she hated the thought of turning fifty. It sounded so old, so terminal. Yes, she missed her children. She was delighted and proud that they were both away studying, but hadn't been prepared to feel so devastated, so untethered, when they left home. And yes, Ted was a good man. Good through and through. Decent and kind and – and Laura was right, she really didn't deserve him. She promised herself she would make more of an effort. Starting from today.

She steered the car into the driveway and got out, admiring the neatly planted front rose beds and the delicate pink clematis that crept along the side wall, just coming into flower. It was a good house; modern, easy to maintain. From the outside it was a bit boxy and square, but once through the door the light flooded in. The large open-plan kitchen-living room-dining area was beautifully stripped back, leading to bifold doors onto the back garden. The interior decoration was vaguely Scandinavian in style; natural wood and stone dominated, with white and mushroom-coloured walls. Yes, she was lucky.

She unlaced her boots and left them by the door, dumped her coat and backpack on a kitchen chair, then walked through to the living area, determined to greet Ted with a smile and ask about his afternoon. Then she stopped. Ted was sitting in his favourite reclining armchair, the newspaper held loosely in his hand. The slippers had fallen from his feet exposing a hole in one sock. His head was tipped back, and his eyes were closed. Gentle snores escaped from his slightly open mouth. Erin struggled to feel the right emotion. She should be feeling fondness, protectiveness, maybe a slight teasing tut-tut of disapproval. Instead she felt the old resentment building up inside her again. It was five in the afternoon, on a Sunday. Her husband was fast asleep, had probably been so for hours, letting the time slip through his slack fingers like grains of sand at the beach. Is this what he wants to do with his life? Sleep it away? As she gazed at his open mouth, showing his slightly crooked teeth and several metal fillings, she was shocked to feel a little stab of distaste. She had a sudden mental image of him sitting in exactly the same position in a care home, with the TV blaring unheeded in a corner. The buzz of restlessness started to build up in her chest once more and she turned away, unable to look at him any longer.

Instead she climbed the stairs to the study and contemplated the telephone. I could call the kids. Find out how they're doing, she thought. But she'd called only a few nights ago. Both Matt and Beth had been happy to chat, but she'd sensed that the calls had been one-sided, her need for contact much greater than theirs. It wasn't fair to call them again. Besides, it had left her feeling unreasonably frustrated as they described their pub sessions, gigs and festival plans. How sad am I to be jealous of my own kids?

She opened the lid of her laptop, but before switching it on she gazed at her reflection in the dark screen. I'm just starting to lose it, she thought. Maybe it's because I'm looking downwards, but my skin looks slack and fleshy around the eyes. She scrunched her blonde hair back tightly with one hand and peered closer, looking for wrinkles. Well, not too bad. Not yet. But how much longer have I got, she thought. How much longer before I disappear into old lady-hood? In ten years I'll probably have grandkids, and that will be OK, great even. It will give me a purpose. I can wear baggy tracksuits, go out make-up-free and take them to the park and I will love that. But how do I survive the next ten years? How can I make it bearable? My life is just a relentless round of work, cooking, TV, sleeping, work, cooking… Broken up with tax bills, car repairs, trips to the dentist. The weeks go by so fast, but there's no real substance to it. No satisfaction. It's all so… soul-destroying. So banal. I feel like I'm disappearing, becoming invisible. There's got to be more to life than that. I want to go out dancing! I want to wear short skirts and heels! I want to travel! I'm so bored. No, that's not even the right word. It's more than boredom. I'm panicky, scared, as if I'm in danger of losing myself. I want to have adventures while I'm still capable! What if I can't make Ted see that? What do I do then? Tears started to fall and she let them drop onto the keyboard. Why can't I be happy? Why can't I be more like Laura?

Erin's thoughts turned back to her sixteenth year, the last time she had felt such a yearning for change. Yes, the accident had been horrific, but there was so much that had been good that year. I wonder what they're all doing now, the old group? They had been a tight little bunch, initially, a kind of family. It would be good to know what they'd become. She turned on the computer and started to idly check her emails and Facebook page. Then, on an impulse, she typed in some of the names which had been floating about in her mind recently. Karen Hill. Millie Smith, Simon… what had been his surname? Laura's warning was forgotten as she tried to find some of the faces she remembered from the past. She found a few possible profiles, and sent out friend requests. For a moment she was lost in her memories. Those early days of fun and laughter. The excitement. The feeling that life was full of possibilities.

It had all started so well…

Chapter Two
December 1988
Just over six months until the accident

Erin trailed into the living room and joined her family. The TV was on. Countryfile, the new series that had just started that year. Oh, for God's sake, she thought. How can anyone watch this boring crap? It's the same stuff every week! Her mother was watching with half an eye as she knitted at the same time. Her hands moved with a speed and sureness born from years of repetition. Her dad seemed genuinely interested in the programme. Must be something about birds, no doubt. Her dad was keen on birds.

'Budge up!' she said to Cathy, as she went to join her on the gold velour sofa. Cathy pulled a displeased face, but shuffled up, leaving space for her older sister. Erin sat down with a thump and sprawled inelegantly on the seat. Her fingers drummed against the armrest.

God, how she hated Sundays. The knowledge that a whole weekend had come and gone too fast. And tomorrow it was the inevitable drudge of school. What had she actually done with her weekend? She'd finished a geography assignment. She'd walked into town with her mum to buy stuff at the market. She'd played a couple of board games with Cathy. She had spent hours in the bathroom, standing on the rim of the bathtub to gaze at her body full-length in the wall mirror opposite, re-learning herself, appraising the new figure which had emerged after weeks and weeks of dieting, holding her hair over her eyes to imagine if she'd look better with a fringe. And that was about it. What a waste of a weekend. She was sixteen years old! Very much a late developer. Some of her schoolfriends had steady boyfriends already. Some had even done it. No, she'd been in the pupal state for far too long. It was time to emerge and fly. But how? Where do you start?

It wasn't fair to blame her family, but blame them she did. Sometimes she positively seethed with unfounded resentment. They were too close, too protective, too much a self-satisfied little unit of four, getting on with life calmly and quietly. She and Cathy had never played outside with other kids, never messed about on bikes. Instead they'd gravitated towards indoor pastimes: painting, reading, even sewing. They were both painfully lacking in street cred. Going to a single-sex school didn't help either; Erin had hardly ever so much as talked to a boy. What did you even talk about? What did boys like? Erin knew something was stirring inside her. She felt it on the way home from school when she walked with excruciating self-awareness past the scrum of boys from the grammar school who were waiting at the bus stop. How could she get their attention? Did she want their attention? How did other girls do it? Should she roll her skirt round its waistband like some of the other girls did, to make her legs look longer? Should she look at them? Smile? Instead she kept her eyes down and hurried past, embarrassed by the depth of her yearning.

I'm sixteen, I'm sixteen, she pleaded, silently. Life should be different by now! I'm missing out! She'd talked to her mother, who'd been sympathetic, but whose response had been 'don't grow up too fast. There's plenty of time, and you'll see, the ones who grow up too fast often make mistakes. Take your time.' That hadn't really helped.

On the TV, the presenter was introducing a ram into a field of ewes, its chest painted a bright orange to later show which ewes had been mounted. Erin turned away in disgust. Even a ram on a farm had a better social life than she did. It wasn't fair.

She grabbed the local newspaper that lay on the coffee table beside the sofa and flicked through the pages, looking for a quick crossword or a horoscope. She skipped past the stories of burglaries and vandalism, the articles on potholes and train delays, until her attention was caught by a photo. A group of half a dozen teenagers were standing in a semi-circle, their arms around each other's shoulders, grinning at the camera. They looked so relaxed, so easy with each other. Three were boys and three were girls. How wonderful to be able to sling your arms round a boy like that, with no second thought, Erin mused. She read the headline: Elm Road Youth Club seeks new members. Elm Road. That wasn't far away. Just the other side of the underpass. Walkable. She read on:

Elm Road Youth Club is open to all young people aged 15 to 20 in the Wakefield area. It is a club run by teenagers, for teenagers, and we aim to provide a social environment for friendship, activities and games. The group meets every Friday evening, from 7pm until 10pm, at the former Elm Road School. Roughly once a month we also aim to organise hikes or camping trips. Activities lined up for this month include silly sports day, talent show and board games night. Come and join us!

Erin stared at the photo, mesmerised. Mentally she placed herself in the semi-circle, imagining how it would feel to be part of this group. They looked nice. Normal. And board games - she was good at them. It didn't sound too scary. This was the push she'd been waiting for. This was a sign, an omen. It was meant to be!

'Mum, Dad, have you seen this?' she asked.

'What's that, love?'

'There's a youth club on Elm Road, and they're looking for new members. It's on Friday nights. Can I go?'

'Let's see.' Her dad reached for the paper and slowly read the article. 'Well it sounds OK. I don't see why not. As long as it doesn't interfere with your school work. Your A-levels must come first.'

Her mother lay down her knitting and took the paper from her husband. 'Friday nights might be OK, I suppose. It'd be nice for you to meet some new people. But it says 'run by teenagers for teenagers'. I'm not sure I like the sound of a youth club without an adult in charge. What do you think, Derek?'

Erin's dad peered over the top of his glasses. 'Um, well if there were some nineteen- or twenty-year-olds, they would count as adults. I think it would be OK.' He gave Erin an almost imperceptible wink.

'Hmm, I suppose. And I'm not so sure about the camping trips either. Not without a parent there to supervise.'

Erin was about to argue, but decided to keep quiet. She would maybe have to fight that battle later.

'It's a pity it's only from age fifteen,' her mother continued. 'Cathy could have gone with you if not. I'd feel better if there were two of you.'

Phew! Thank God for the age limit, Erin thought, discretely crossing her fingers behind her back. There was no way she wanted her annoying little sister hanging around. She had a better idea.

'What about if Laura came too? I know she lives miles away, but it's on a Friday so she could stay the night and get the bus home in the morning. Couldn't she?'

'We'll see, dear, we'll see. Don't get ahead of yourself. We'd need to speak to Laura's parents first.'

'Can I phone her? Please?'

'Well, OK.' Her dad was smiling at her eagerness but her mother had pursed her lips. Erin knew she was having doubts. Maybe about safety? Or more probably about the impact on her study routine. Erin knew she would have to get her father alone and subtly work him over to her side, let him be the one to convince her mum.

She left the room and went into the dark hallway. The telephone stood on a little side-table near the front door. It was freezing in the hallway; the cold seeped up from the Victorian tiled floor and Erin wished she had her slippers on. Their house was impressive enough from the outside, she supposed; detached, with double-fronted bay windows and mature chestnut trees which tapped against the bedroom windows at night. Inside was a different matter; the family had to put up with unreliable Victorian plumbing and tall, single-glazed sash windows. The surface of Erin's bedcover was often damp with condensation on cold winter mornings, and little fern-shaped trails of ice would build up on the inside of her window panes. When the wind howled outside, it somehow found its way under the foundations, making the carpets lift and bubble up from the living room floor. It was a family joke to ignore the shifting carpets when rare visitors called round, and to secretly watch their confusion as they wondered if they had drunk too much sherry. Yes, it was a fine, stately old house, but Erin would have gladly swapped for Laura's modern semi in the little village several miles out of town. She imagined Laura now in her cosy central-heated living room. I bet she's nice and warm. She dialled the number.

'Laura, guess what! There's a youth club near my house and they want to find new members. And we could both join, couldn't we, and it's on Friday nights, and you could stay over at our house. What do you say? You've got to say yes! Please, please?'

***

The next morning, Erin woke up with a new sense of purpose. The usual feelings of dread at the thought of another school week had receded, and Erin walked the half-mile to school with a new spring in her step. In the breaks Laura and Erin talked earnestly about Friday night, wondering what to wear, planning how Laura could bring a change of clothes to school, whether they could safely walk home afterwards through the underpass, or whether Erin's dad would give them a lift, as Laura's parents preferred.

'Our lives are about to change, you'll see,' said Erin, her face alight with optimism. 'We'll have things to do. Reasons to get out of the house. We'll be like the cool kids!'

'Yeah, great!' said Laura, although she secretly doubted she would ever be classified as 'cool'.

Their lives did indeed change that year. Massively. But not in the way either of them had hoped for. Change can be exciting, invigorating. But change can also be confusing, unsettling – and sometimes downright dangerous.

Chapter Three
Six months until the accident

Erin's dad dropped them off at the end of the road, and the two girls approached the old school with a mixture of excitement and trepidation. They had built this moment up in their heads into something extraordinary, and were scared it would be a let-down. They followed the low stone wall to the entrance gateposts and paused. The former school building towered above them; grimy grey bricks and rows of long, narrow windows gave it a prison-like feel. The roof line was made up of three separate peaks, and above these stood a pollution-stained cupola. There were two entrances, one at each end of the building, with doors painted a dull institutional green. The first entrance had 'BOYS' and the second had 'GIRLS' carved in blackened capitals into the stone lintels above. The playground in front was tarmacked, but clumps of weeds were breaking through to reclaim their space. A weathered sign with 'Elm Road Community Centre' painted in peeling blue letters had fallen from its support and lay propped up against a wall. It was a dismal-looking building, so different from their own modern school, and their spirits plummeted. They paused with their hands on the gate and listened. They could hear voices coming from somewhere behind the school buildings. Laughter. Then a shriek.

'Come on!' said Erin, a little grimly. 'We're here now.'

They followed the wall round two sides of the old building,

until they came to a small playing field. Two boys were throwing a frisbee to each other at the far end of the field, one tall, fair and solidly built, the other very slight, dark-skinned and quick on his feet. Nearest to them, an overweight boy was kneeling on the ground and occasionally looking up, smiling at the other two boys, as he sorted through what looked like a pile of old clothes. A girl with messy blonde hair was jumping around excitedly, trying to wrest a balloon from a second, taller, dark-haired girl who twisted away then held the balloon up high. Both were contorted with laughter. Out of the school building came a third girl, with short brown hair cut in a pudding-bowl style and thick-lensed glasses. She was carrying a tin bucket and several paper cups. As she caught sight of the two girls, she put the bucket and cups on the ground and came rushing over. She reminded Erin of a little sparrow, with her short, pecking steps and bustling manner.

'Hello, hello! Have we got some new members?'

'Um, yes, if that's OK. Can we join in today and see what it's like?' asked Laura.

'Yes, of course. That's brilliant! We need more people today. I'm Fiona. What are your names?'

'I'm Erin.'

'And I'm Laura.'

'Welcome to the group! It's great that you're here. Did you see the article in the Express? We used to be a much bigger group, but lots of the older ones have gone off to university this year, or got jobs and stuff, so…so we're a bit short of members just now. Anyway, let me tell you about us. We meet every Friday and do different things. Today it's crazy relay races. Next week is quiz night. Then we've got scavenger hunt, karaoke night, um… what else? We charge a pound per night for subs, and that goes towards buying things like tea and coffee, biscuits, or other stuff we need. Every fourth week we have a meeting to organise the programme for the next month and we all vote on the best idea… so if you've got any good ideas, that would be great and…'

As Fiona went on to talk about the responsibilities of setting up the room and clearing up afterwards, turning off the lights and locking up, her eyes magnified and earnest behind her thick, round-framed glasses, Erin found her attention drifting. The two boys with the frisbee were walking across the field towards them. The taller one was quite good-looking, she decided.

Gradually the other members also wandered over to join them, and Fiona made the introductions.

'Everyone, this is Laura. And this is Erin. They've come for a try-out. This is Hamza. He's football mad.' She pointed to the dark-skinned boy, who grinned shyly. 'And this is Tom. He's the brainy one.' Tom, the tall frisbee thrower, gave a little salute and said 'Hi.' 'And this is Millie, she's the youngest, she's fourteen and shouldn't really be here, but we let her. She's nuts.' Millie looked even younger than fourteen, with her wide-apart blue eyes and a frizz of blonde hair. Erin felt a momentary pang of guilt, thinking of Cathy, also fourteen years old, stuck at home with her parents. But tough, this was going to be her thing, not Cathy's.

'And finally, this is Karen. She's the sporty one.' Karen turned to smile at them. She had beautiful bone structure; high cheekbones, a delicate nose, pointed chin and glossy brown hair that was caught up in a high pony tail – but her face was marred by acne, which she had tried to disguise with heavy foundation and concealer. Erin quickly masked her initial shock and gave her a warm smile.

'Hey, what about me?' came a voice from the back of the group. A third boy pushed his way gently to the front. His thighs and arms were enormous. His lank hair needed a wash and the t-shirt that strained across his chest was not too clean.

'Oh, Gosh, sorry,' said Fiona. 'This is Simon. He's everybody's favourite. So, right. Let's get started! Karen, we need six balloons. Can you blow some more up? Simon, can you sort the clothes into two equal piles. Tom and Hamza, we need something to mark the start and end of the tracks. Can you find something?'

'What can we do?' asked Laura.
'Can you fill up the bucket? There's an outside tap over there.'

**

That first Friday was a triumph. Erin's dad smiled as he watched the two girls coming through the schoolyard gate just after ten o'clock that night. They were arm-in-arm and rather dirty, but both girls' faces were alive with excitement. They looked so happy, so vibrant as they walked towards the car. Beautiful. He felt a sudden pang, realising that his daughter was growing up, changing, no longer a child.

'How was it?' he asked, rather needlessly.

'Dad, it was brilliant! We did lots of silly relay races, it was amazing!'

'Oh yeah? What kind of races?'

'Um, there was one where you have to hold a frisbee between your knees and hop to the next person and pass it to them.'

'No, I thought the best one was the clothes race,' said Laura. 'You had to run to the end of the field, put on a hat, a dress, scarf, coat, then run back and take it all off for the next person.'

'Oh, I know that one,' said Erin's dad. 'We used to do that when I was a lad.'

'And there was a balloon one. We had two teams of four and there were three balloons between us, at chest height, but you couldn't touch them. You had to squeeze together and all walk up the field without the balloons falling.'

Erin prattled on, knowing that her dad would be reassured by the rather childish games, and would relay his opinion that the youth club was innocent and respectable to her mother. She neglected to tell him about the last game. As the light began to fade they had returned inside the old school building to play sardines in the musty classrooms. One person was sent to hide, and whenever someone found that person they had squeeze into the same place, until the last person found them all. Erin was glad her dad couldn't see her, now, in the back seat of the car.

She knew she was blushing as she remembered being squashed in the former stationary cupboard between Hamza and Simon, then squashed still further together as Karen joined them. She had never been this close to a boy before. Hamza's thigh was hard against hers and she felt his breath on her cheek. She could smell the sweat emanating from Simon on her other side. They held their breath and listened to footsteps pacing the corridor outside. Then the door was flung open and Tom appeared. He had pushed himself into the tight space and closed the door quickly. Erin's whole body was suddenly and shockingly in contact with his. Her nose was pressed against his chest and she inhaled the smell of his wool jumper. She could feel the buckle of his belt against her stomach. She was intensely aware that he would be able to feel the soft mounds of her breasts. She wondered if he was able to smell her newly washed hair, too. Every nerve in her body seemed to be hyper-sensitive, tingling, alert. She felt as if she might explode with some strange, new and raw emotion.

'And what were the other people like?' asked Erin's dad now, breaking the spell and returning Erin's thoughts to the present. 'Were they nice?'

'Nice. Very, very nice,' said Erin, thinking of one particular person. He was very nice indeed.

***

The next two months were some of the happiest Erin had ever experienced. As the weeks passed, she knew she'd turned a corner. She felt herself opening up like a plant, kept for too long indoors on a windowsill, and now suddenly transplanted outside into the spring sunshine. She was unfolding, pushing out tentative new shoots, reaching up towards the light. She threw away the baggy t-shirts and comfortable jeans which no longer fitted her. That was her old life, those were her cover-up clothes. She began to relax into her newly slim body, and to cautiously show it off, spending some of her precious savings on straight-legged jeans and fitted tops. Her blonde hair, which she'd previously worn scraped back severely into a low ponytail, was now loose and layered after a visit to the hairdresser, and curled pleasingly about her ears each time she turned her head. She started wearing mascara, and, much to her mother's disapproval, went into town one morning to get her ears pierced. 'Oh, you silly girl!' her mother had complained. 'I do think that looks common.' But Erin was not listening. It was no longer a mother's approval that she craved or needed. She was amazed and intoxicated by her new appearance. She couldn't stop looking at herself in mirrors and shop windows, thinking: Is that really me? She no longer scuttled, head down and shoulders hunched, past the boys at the bus stop. Instead she held her head high and lengthened her stride. I've got friends! I'm in a group! I don't need you spotty grammar school boys any more. And where Erin led, Laura faithfully followed. The two girls spent hours poring over magazines for make-up tips and scouring the market stalls for cheap new clothes at the weekend. The world had suddenly become a voyage of discovery. Possibilities were unlimited!

Both lived for Friday nights, when they would push open the door of the old school building and be greeted by this mixed bunch of interesting, non-judgemental people. The activities were almost always fun, - karaoke, quizzes, tug of war - but for Erin, the best part of each session was the end, when the group would sit around on hard wooden school chairs in a corner of the old assembly hall, as the sun sank behind the trees outside. As the room grew gradually darker, inhibitions seemed to melt away and an atmosphere of protective intimacy reigned. The group began with chat and jokes, but as evening turned to night, they often opened up to each other, confessing their deepest fears and secret hopes for the future.

Gradually Erin and Laura got to know and appreciate the different members of the group. On a rare night when everyone turned up there were twelve teenagers, but some of the members

- especially the older ones - only came now and again. The core consisted of just six people, and they became the centre of Erin's world. Hamza was the quietest, usually sitting a little way off and listening to the others, rarely contributing. After a little gentle probing, he admitted one night that his parents wanted him to study medicine, but he himself dreamed of becoming a professional footballer. He was scared of disappointing his parents, but also worried that he'd never grow tall enough to be a footballer.

Millie reminded Erin of a newly-hatched, brightly coloured butterfly, landing on each person for a few seconds before fluttering off to the next. She was wide-eyed, scatty and excitable. Her hands moved constantly but clumsily as she talked – but her words were often complete nonsense and she had an endearing habit of getting her facts mixed up. Her enthusiasm bordered on the manic at times; she hated the activities to end and would beg them for 'just one more go' or 'we can't stop yet!' At other times she could be morose, sulky and petulant, and Erin wondered if she could possibly be bi-polar. Because of her age, she was treated as the unofficial mascot of the group and everyone looked out for her.

Fiona was earnest and well-meaning, older than her seventeen years. There was no elected leader of the group, but if there had been, Fiona would definitely have been it. She kept everyone on their toes, reminding them whose turn it was to wash up, collecting the subs and efficiently chairing the monthly planning meetings. When someone told a joke she would look up through her milk-bottle lenses and say 'sorry, I don't get it.' The others would laugh and explain the punchline, but with no hint of mockery. Fiona was deeply religious and always wore a little gold cross around her neck. On several occasions she would try to bring the discussion round to faith, which the others gently steered her away from. But when someone talked about a problem, Fiona inevitably said: 'I'll pray for you tonight; it'll be OK.' And that person usually found it strangely comforting.

Erin felt a special bond with Karen, who was tall and athletic with a sharp wit. Her face was pitted with acne, which she tried, and failed, to cover up with concealer. Karen admitted one Friday night that she was getting bullied continuously by a clique of girls at her school. They called her names like 'crater face', 'freak' and 'elephant girl' and turned their backs when she approached. The group had hugged her and told her that the acne would pass, and that one day she would be more beautiful than all those bitchy girls at school.

Erin also had a tremendous soft spot for Simon, one of the oldest in the group at nineteen. He was a gentle giant of a boy who had a difficult home life, having to care for a sick mother. He never mentioned a father, or siblings. Food had obviously become his comfort and reward, and he was an unhealthy weight, but no-one in the group teased him for his size. They understood that Friday nights were a rare break in the week for him. He was generous-spirited, and being the only one with a car, he would offer a lift to anyone who needed one for the days out. He quickly offered to give Erin and Laura a lift home every Friday night to avoid Erin's dad having to come out, and made a point of introducing himself to Erin's parents to reassure them.

And then there was Tom. Perfect Tom. Tall, laconic and handsome in an understated way, with a straight nose, a direct gaze and wavy blonde hair which flopped over one eye. He reminded Erin of the young World War Two fighter pilots she'd seen in black-and-white films on TV; unassuming, stoical, leaning against the wall with his hands in his pockets. He was just missing the cigarette in the corner of his mouth. In her head, she built him the character that his natural reticence prevented him from showing.

'Do you fancy Tom?' Laura asked her one day at school. They were sitting on a bench outside the sixth-form common room, waiting for the bell to ring. The two girls generally got through the endless boredom of school days by dissecting each moment of the previous Friday's meeting, and by discussing each group member obsessively, but this was the first time Laura had asked this question.

'Yes, of course. He's gorgeous! Why, don't you?'

'Um, no, not really. I mean, he's really nice, but not in a very sexy way. More of an older brother way. No, I like Hamza. He's got such beautiful dark eyes.'

'Oh, do you? I think Tom's really cool. Do you think he likes me?'

'Um… hard to tell. He doesn't say much, does he?'

'But he looks at me a lot. Do you think I should ask him out?'

'God, I don't know. It might be really awkward if he says no.'

'Yeah, that's true. I'm not sure if I'm brave enough for that. Not unless he gives some kind of sign that he likes me.'

As it happened, Erin didn't have to ask Tom out. At the end of one Friday session, having not spoken to her all night, Tom came up to her and blurted out:

'Do you want to go to the cinema with me next week?'

'Oh! Um, um…Yes, OK.'

'Good. I'll phone you.' Then he was gone.

The following week they sat together, not touching, in the crowded cinema, watching a rather stupid science fiction movie and eating popcorn from the same carton. Each time their hands accidentally met, Erin felt a thrilling jolt of electricity. When the film ended, Tom offered to walk her home. They discussed the film briefly, but after that, grew silent. When they reached her front gate he suddenly leant down and kissed her quickly and clumsily on the mouth, before saying 'Bye. See you on Friday,' and hurrying away down the street.

Erin went to bed that night thinking that her world could not be more perfect. She hugged her pillow and thought about the kiss, replaying it over and over in her mind. Admittedly it was not quite what she'd anticipated for her first kiss, but it was a kiss nevertheless. She had been on a date! She would have a boyfriend! They would go out together!

Erin was right to treasure those two golden months and that special night with Tom.

Because the following Friday a new member appeared in the group.

The solid ground that Erin had believed she was standing on was nothing but thin ice. And cracks would soon start to show.

Chapter Four

Now

'Can you chuck me Dudley's towel, Richard?' called Laura. She held onto the dog's collar with one hand, pushing open the porch door with the other. Dudley strained against her hand, anxious to get back into the warmth of the house.

Richard ambled into the porch and laughed.

'Oh God, he's covered! Should we throw him in the bath?'

'No, poor old Dudley, he hates the bath. We'll just get the worst off.'

Richard's knees gave an audible crack as he knelt down and took each paw in turn, gently rubbing between the delicate pads and removing what mud he could. Then he vigorously rubbed the dog's body, making Dudley squirm with pleasure. Once released, Dudley ambled off on stiff legs to find his favourite spot under the living room radiator. Laura took off her muddy boots, hung up her coat, and they both went into the kitchen.

'Cuppa?'

'Please.'

'Where did you get to today?' asked Richard, filling the kettle.

'We met up in the pub car park at Stanley Ferry, then walked along the canal towpath to the Washlands reserve. It was quite easy going on the towpath, but the Washlands was really muddy and slippery. It's a good walk though. Not too long. We should do it together sometime.'

'And how was Erin today?'

Laura pulled a face. 'Oh, you know... she's still in one of her moods. I thought she'd have snapped out of it by now.'

'Is she still bored?'

'I'd say restless more than bored. She gets these black periods when nothing is ever enough. Whatever she has, she always wants more. I don't know what to say to her any more. I can't get through to her and I'm getting fed up with it.'

'I'm sure. Is it just the menopause, do you think?'

'Could be. But she's always been a bit like that.'

'How is Ted coping with it?'

'Well, that's the thing. She kind of blames Ted for her restlessness. Thinks he should be more active, more energetic. I'm worried she's going to leave him!'

'Really? That bad? Poor Ted.'

'I know.'

'Well, you know my thoughts about Erin. I find her very hard to take. She's selfish. I've seen how your friendship works over the years; you run whenever she calls, you bend over backwards for her. But it doesn't seem to work the other way. I don't think she's even aware that you might have your own problems. It seems an unequal kind of relationship to me.'

'I know, you're probably right. But she's my oldest friend. We were at kindergarten together. I know her better than anyone – except you, of course. I can't just drop her.'

'But could you maybe... I don't know... make her work for it a bit more? Like this morning; she rang, she wanted to talk, she was feeling bad, and you dropped everything – which meant that I had to take Nathan to football yet again. I don't mind, but... if you said 'no' now and again it might make her take you less for granted.'

'You're right. I find that hard though, it's not in my nature.' Laura took a long gulp of tea. 'I might have to keep my distance from her for a bit though, for my own self-preservation. She's talking some scary shit at the moment.'

'Really? What like?'

'She keeps harking back to the old days, the youth club days, the time before the accident. I think she wants to get back in contact with those people again.'

'Would that be so bad?'

Lura pulled a face. 'For me, yes. I was in therapy for about a year after the accident, trying to process it all. It's something I think I've managed to come to terms with, but I don't want to risk opening it all up again.'

'You never really talk about the accident. All I know is that one of your friends died. Do you want to talk about it now?'

'Not really.' Laura sighed. 'You know what happened. A bunch of us went camping. We walked up to the top of Malham Cove. The weather was crap and the rocks were slippery and...'

'And someone fell.'

'Yes,' said Laura in a whisper. 'It was my first experience of death and it was awful.' She stayed silent for a long moment, staring out of the kitchen window with unseeing eyes. Then she continued in a stronger voice. 'Erin and I had to identify the body. They drove us to the hospital mortuary and showed us into this tiny room. We were clinging onto each other, trying to be brave. They pulled the sheet down to the chin and... oh God!' She shivered. 'They tried to shield us from the worst of it, they warned us, but you could tell that half the face was just... mashed, pulped. And the eyes. They were gone. I threw up.'

Richard came round the table, put an arm round Laura and kissed the top of her head. 'I think it's criminal, what they did,' he said, angry at what she'd had to go through. 'They should never have asked you; you were too young. They should have waited for a family member to do it. It must have been horrific.'

'I don't think they could find anyone from the family. They asked us if one of us would do it. Erin was the only one brave enough. She said yes and I couldn't let her do it alone. But I wish we hadn't.'

'But you were, what? Sixteen? Is that not against the law or something?'

'I think she might have told them she was older. I don't know. Anyway, it ended up being us.'

'Do you think that's why you went into nursing? Because you saw that death when you were young and it made you want to save people?'

'I never thought of that. But yes, it makes sense.'

'Anyway, don't think about it any more. It's all in the past and can't hurt you now. Let's talk about something else. What shall we eat tonight? Shall we get fish and chips? Or a curry? Nathan's going out so we can have a relaxing evening, find something to watch on Netflix. Do you fancy watching...'

But Laura was not listening. She saw again the damaged body under the white sheet. She remembered the mortuary attendant's kindness as he'd handed her tissues and led her back down the corridor. Her parents' shocked faces when they came to fetch her. She remembered her weekly visits to the therapist's room with its pale wallpaper and bland seascape paintings. Almost one year of therapy. One year to pinpoint the root of her trauma.

And it hadn't been the shock of experiencing a teenage death. It hadn't been the recurring images of the broken body on the mortuary table. No, that wasn't what had plagued her the most.

No, the root of her trauma was guilt.

Chapter Five
Four months until the accident

'Oh, you've brought a guitar!' said Tom, stating the obvious. 'I didn't know you played.'

'I'm not very good. I've only been learning for a while,' said Erin. She didn't want to raise expectations, but she'd been practicing the introduction from Stairway To Heaven for days now, and was almost note perfect. 'What are you going to do?'

'A card trick. It was all I could think of.'

'I'm sure it'll be great.' Erin smiled her encouragement. 'Laura couldn't think of anything either. She's going to recite this lame poem we had to learn by heart years ago at school.'

It was talent night at the group, one of Fiona's ideas, and Erin and Laura were not particularly looking forward to it. Hamza was going to try and beat his record for keepy-uppies, and Karen would probably amaze them with backflips and handsprings. An older member called Bob was laying out some grainy black-and-white photos he'd taken of Wakefield – graffiti on the prison walls, abandoned kebabs in doorways, TO LET signs on boarded-up shop fronts. Millie was hiding in the kitchen area, doing something secretive with dressing up clothes, and Simon had not yet arrived. Fiona hurried over to distribute paper and pens for scoring.

'Crikey, it's just like Eurovision,' muttered Erin, and Tom gave a snort of agreement. 'Let's make a pact to give each other full marks, however crap it goes.'

Just a normal Friday night, relaxed and jokey. Things were a little slow to get underway. Simon finally arrived and Fiona clapped her hands to bring things to order.

And that's when the door opened and the new girl walked in.

Erin didn't notice at first, sitting opposite Tom, with her back to the entrance. But gradually she became aware that a kind of stunned silence had descended on the room. Tom's face had gone slack and his mouth had fallen slightly open.

She turned and gave an involuntary gasp.

The girl was extraordinary. She stood tall and straight, but conveyed a certain languid elegance. A motorbike helmet was looped around the crook of one arm. Her blonde hair was long and messy and bleached white at the tips. She was wearing wide jeans, low on her waist and ripped at the knee, a black t-shirt left loose and a red-and-black man's plaid shirt over the top. Her feet were encased in purple Doc Martens and her nail polish was as black as her eyeliner. She held herself with extraordinary self-confidence, almost defiance, as she looked around the room.

Erin was suddenly aware of her own clothes; a neat pair of high-waisted, ankle-length jeans with a tight yellow t-shirt tucked in at the waist – the fashion uniform of most of her friends, inspired by Kylie or pre-wedding Diana. The clothes she was so proud of suddenly seemed much too safe, too conventional.

Fiona hurried over and started to give her usual welcome speech.

'Hello, are you a new member?' The girl just stared at her, coolly, unblinking. 'Um, let me tell you about the group. We meet on Friday evenings and...' Throughout the speech, the girl fixed Fiona with expressionless green eyes, and Fiona started to falter.

'Um, where was I? Um, yes, we charge one pound in subs and...' She broke off suddenly, as the girl lazily reached into her shirt pocket and took out a packet of cigarettes.

'You can't smoke in here!' squeaked Fiona, horrified.

The girl gave a sudden wide smile, showing even white teeth, but the smile did not reach her eyes.

'Really? Whatever,' she said, shrugging and putting the pack back in her pocket. 'My name's Tara. Tara Blake.'

'Oh. Right. Yes. Um, well, I'm Fiona. Let me introduce you to the rest of the group.'

The girl followed Fiona round the room, giving a nod and a cool stare as she was presented to Laura, then Millie. Only when introduced to Karen did she speak:

'Jesus, what happened to your face? Have you had chicken pox?'

'No, it's acne.' Karen muttered, cheeks aflame, and Erin cringed in sympathy.

'No shit!' said Tara, unperturbed. 'Bummer.'

'This is Tom, and this is Hamza.'

Erin watched in fascination as the boys reacted differently to the new member. Hamza stared at the floor. He seemed to deflate and fade further into the distance as if trying to make himself invisible. Tom, on the other hand, couldn't peel his eyes away from her. Erin was not overly surprised; she felt a bit the same way herself. Only Simon reacted normally, smiling and saying 'Hi.'

'And this is Erin.'

'Hello,' said Erin. Was it her imagination, or did Tara look at her with just a little hint of interest, a smile twitching her lips, before saying 'Hi' back? Had she been singled out in some way?

Erin found the rest of the evening excruciating. She suddenly found herself looking at the group with new eyes, critical eyes. The eyes of this stranger. Fiona stood up and sang Amazing Grace very well, hitting the high notes easily, but her wide-eyed earnestness, her total lack of self-awareness was so painful that Erin could hardly bear to watch. Laura stumbled through her poem as quickly as she could and sat down again, relieved. Millie performed a kind of stand-up routine that was unrehearsed and jumbled, impossible to follow. Erin played her guitar piece well enough, but felt no pride or enjoyment. Throughout all the performances she was aware of the new girl, Tara, looking on impassively. 'We're a bunch of misfits' thought Erin, shocked by her sudden insight. 'No hopers. We're not cool at all!' She looked around the room at the people she had idolised over the past weeks. Laura was slouching on a chair, wearing a boxy t-shirt and scuffed trainers, her glorious auburn hair scraped back and tied with a rubber band. Why didn't she make more of herself? Fiona, with her unflattering pageboy haircut, round glasses and quick, sharp movements. She was an old woman in a child's body. Simon, genial, kindly Simon – he looked a bit of a mess, frankly, as if he needed a good wash. Millie, with her hair sticking up all over the place – a kid. What must this new girl think of us all?

When everyone had done their piece, Fiona walked up to Tara, a hesitant smile on her face, and asked:

'Do you want to do something? Have you got a special talent you can show us?'

'I've got many talents,' said Tara, her mouth curling in a half-smile as she stood up lazily. 'Can I see your hand?' Before waiting for an answer she reached for Fiona's hand and took it in hers, palm upwards. With one finger she traced the lines. 'You will marry young and I see one child. Your lifeline is truncated. I see...'

Fiona snatched her hand away with a gasp. 'What are you doing? You can't do that! It's not... I don't believe... I'm a Christian!'

Tara laughed. 'Yes, I can see you're a good God-fearing girl. You're wearing his little sign.' She pointed at the cross.

'Well, aren't you?'

Tara grinned wickedly, her eyes gleaming. 'Not me. I'm a pagan.'

Fiona took two steps back, horrified. 'You're kidding, right?'

'Maybe. Maybe not.'

Fiona stared at her for a moment, then hurried away to collect the votes. She looked flustered, off-balance. Tara shrugged and sat down again, choosing a chair next to Erin.

'Did you say that thing about being a pagan just to wind Fiona up?' Erin whispered to her.

Tara just shrugged again.

'Can you really read people's palms?'

In reply, Tara surreptitiously lifted Erin's hand, scrutinised it quickly and announced: 'You and I are going to be friends.'

Erin felt a current of electricity pass between them. She had been singled out! She was interesting to this girl. As she smiled back, she caught a glimpse of Laura, sitting opposite and staring back at her. Her mouth was set in a firm line.

Fiona counted the scores and Hamza was declared the winner. He looked down modestly as the others whooped and applauded. Erin noticed that Tara didn't clap.

'Is this the kind of thing you do every week?' Tara asked her.

'Um, well, no, we do lots of different things. Karaoke, quizzes, sports challenges. So what do you think? Did you like it?' asked Erin.

The girl gave Erin a direct stare. 'Honestly? It's a bit crap isn't it? It feels more like being back at Girl Guides - or Brownies. I was expecting something a bit more grown up. But maybe I'll come back next week. I don't know.' She shrugged. 'I'll see.'

With that, she collected her crash helmet, turned her back to them all and headed for the door, flipping one hand back in a casual goodbye as she left the room.

There was a palpable release of tension and everyone started talking at once.

'Bloody hell! She didn't stay and help clear up!'

'Where did she come from? I'm sure she doesn't go to our school. Does she go to the comp?'

'Never seen her there.'

'I don't think she'll come back, she doesn't fit in.'

'She seemed really snotty. I hope she doesn't.'

'Oh, I don't know. Maybe we need someone new to give us

some new ideas.'

'D'you think she's really a pagan?'

'Nah, she was just talking bollocks.'

As Laura and Erin stacked the chairs at the back of the room, they continued to discuss the new girl.

'What did you think of her?' asked Erin.

'Huh! I did not like her one little bit. Did you hear what she said to Karen? And how she looked down her nose at us all? And I heard her say 'shove up, lard-arse' to Simon. That's pretty mean.'

'Oh, I don't know, I thought she was kind of cool. Very sure of herself. Not really giving a crap what we all thought. I sometimes wish I was more like that.'

'No you don't. That's not cool, that's arrogance. Anyway, she won't come back. She's way too edgy for us lot.'

But she did come back. Week after week. And fracture lines slowly began to appear in the group.

Chapter Six
Three months until the accident

'Where did you get those jeans?' asked Laura, a couple of weeks later as they got ready in Erin's enormous bathroom. It was the coldest room in the house, the big sash window didn't close properly and the radiator was barely tepid. They stood shoulder to shoulder, peering into the cloudy antique mirror as they inexpertly applied blue eye-shadow.

'On the market, where else? D'you like them?'

'Not much, to be honest.' Laura took a step back and took in Erin's attire. She frowned. 'Are you copying Tara's style now? I didn't know you liked ripped jeans.'

'No, it's nothing to do with Tara,' said Erin, a little defensively. 'It's the new fashion. It's called grunge. I'm just keeping up with the trend.'

'Oh yeah? And is that eyeliner you're putting on now? Black eyeliner?'

'So?' Erin felt herself growing hot.

'What's next, the black nail polish too? Doc Martens? Have you got a girl crush?'

'No I have not! Don't be stupid. I'm just experimenting a bit.' Erin didn't dare admit she'd already started saving up for Doc Martens. Burgundy, not purple. That wasn't copying.

'Look, I just don't think Tara's a very nice person. You shouldn't idolise her.'

Erin was suddenly furious. 'I'm not idolising anyone!' she snapped. 'What's the matter with you? Can't I try out a new style? We're not twins. We don't always have to be the same.'

'No, you're right. We're not the same,' said Laura, quietly.

They finished doing their make-up in uncomfortable silence. Laura pulled the rubber band from her ponytail, brushed her glossy auburn hair, then tied it back up again.

'You should leave it loose,' said Erin. 'Your hair's such a lovely colour. I wish I had your hair.'

Laura recognised the peace signals, but didn't respond. They went downstairs, called goodbye to Erin's parents and left the house. As they walked through the underpass, holding their breath to avoid the smell of piss and vomit, Erin felt a wave of remorse. She'd known Laura since they were both four years old; they never fell out.

'Sorry for snapping earlier on,' she said when they emerged once more onto the street. 'I suppose I am copying her a bit. I just like what she wears. It doesn't mean I like her necessarily. You'll always be my best friend.'

'Should bloody well think so,' said Laura, punching her lightly on the arm. 'We've been friends forever. Anyway, what about Tom? Are you two going out, or what?'

'Um... it's all gone a bit quiet. We've been out three times now, but he's never tried to kiss me again. And he hasn't phoned for over a week now. I don't think it's going anywhere.'

'Oh, I'm sorry. You really liked him.'

'To be honest, I'm not sure I'm that bothered. He seems to be more into Tara now, always following her around like a little puppy-dog. So no, I'm not really that upset. Besides, he's a rubbish kisser.'

'How would you know? Have you got anyone to compare him to?'

'I just know. It's got to be better than that. Come on, let's hurry, we're going to be late.'

They picked up their pace and chatted companionably once

again, until they reached Elm Road. Pushing open the gate, they saw Tara and Millie leaning against the school wall, their heads together. Hearing the gate twang shut, Millie looked up with a rather sly expression, and handed something quickly back to Tara. A roll-up.

'Have you been smoking?' Laura demanded, marching up to Millie and giving her a hard stare. Then she turned to Tara. 'She's only fourteen, you know. You shouldn't encourage her to smoke!'

'Whatever,' replied Tara, nonchalantly. 'I was smoking when I was twelve. But whatever.' She crushed the cigarette out with the toe of her Doc Marten, flicked it away, and the four of them walked towards the door. Laura caught a strange, sweet smell as she followed them in. Tobacco didn't smell like that, did it? Was that weed? Marijuana? Surely not. She pulled Erin back and whispered:

'I think it might have been marijuana in that roll-up! She's making Millie smoke dope!'

'No, surely not. Anyway, would you know how to recognise that? I think it's probably just that rolling tobacco. It smells different from ordinary cigarettes. Come on, don't get all dramatic.'

She pushed past Laura and entered the assembly hall. Inside, the others were standing in a circle around Fiona, who was sitting on a chair with pen and paper in hand.

'Hold on, hold on, you're all talking at once. If we each suggest one item, that's fair,' she said. 'Karen, what's yours?'

'A feather.'

'OK, good.' Fiona wrote it down. 'Tom?'

'Beer mat.' Fiona looked a bit disapproving, but added it to the list. She glanced up as the late-comers joined the group.

'What's the deal here?' asked Tara.

'It's the scavenger hunt tonight, don't you remember?' said Fiona, irritated. 'I gave everyone the month's new programme last week. We've got almost all the items: pine cone, white stone, take-away menu, empty crisp packet, bus ticket, feather, beer mat, something purple – we need one more.'

'Let's jazz things up. Something a little risky,' said Tara, with a half-smile. 'Road sign.'

'What do you mean, road sign? You mean pinch one? We can't do that!' Fiona was aghast.

'Yep. Oh, come on, Fiona! Your list is so tame. Live a little! Have you never stolen anything?'

'No I have not! And I'm not going to start now.'

'Oh, but it's fun. Christ, how old are you? A hundred?' Tara sniggered.

'I think we should put the road sign in. Or a traffic cone. Either one,' said Tom.

'It's illegal. You could get a fine. And a police record.'

'I've always wanted a traffic cone in my bedroom.' He glanced at Tara for approval and Erin rolled her eyes and thought 'you suck-up'.

Fiona looked around the group uncertainly, gauging the mood. Simon was smiling. Hamza just shrugged. Millie looked over-excited, as usual. Fiona knew her authority was being challenged and she didn't know how to react. This hadn't happened before and she didn't like it.

'All right then, I'll put it on the list, but if anyone gets caught, you don't mention the group. You're on your own. Right. Teams of two, and one team of three. Who's with who?'

Laura looked at Erin expectantly; they always paired up for activities, but before she could speak, Tara jumped in.

'Let's break things up a bit,' she said, looking coolly at Laura. 'We're always in the same teams. I know, what about Laura with Hamza.' Oh, that's nice, thought Erin. She knows Laura likes him. She won't disagree to that. 'Bob with Andrew and Simon - we'll put the three oldies together. Fiona with Millie. Karen with Tom. I'll go with Erin? OK?'

And so it was decided. As Fiona carefully made copies of the list, Laura pulled Erin aside.

'That was clever,' she said.

'What was?'

'I think Tara's trying to break us up. I know she doesn't like me.'

'Oh, Laura! Stop being so sensitive! It's just a game. Come on, you'll have a great time with Hamza all to yourself. This is your big chance! You can really get to know him.'

Fiona distributed the lists and told everyone to be back in an hour and a half maximum. They all exited the building. Millie waited as Fiona locked the door. Karen and Tom headed off towards the park, and Laura and Hamza walked quickly in the other direction, towards the town centre.

'Right then,' said Tara. 'Pub. Let's go to The Bull.'

'Oh, OK,' said Erin. 'Beer mat. Good idea.' She knew The Bull was one of Wakefield's most disreputable pubs, located near the high-security jail and rumoured to be a place to score drugs. But it was close, and they'd be able to knock the first item off the list quickly. But when they entered, Tara surprised her.

'Grab that seat. I'll get the drinks.'

'What? I thought we were just here for the beer mat?'

'We'll get that too. Go on, sit down.'

'But what about the scavenger hunt? We'll waste too much time if we have a drink here.'

'Erin, chill out. You've got to start listening to your true feelings. Don't just do what's expected of you all the time. You don't have to conform. Listen. What do you really want to do right now; go out on the street and pick up a load of crappy shit, or sit here and talk to me?'

'Oh, well, I suppose…'

Tara smiled. She knew she'd won. She turned to the barman. 'Two pints of bitter please.'

Erin took a seat and looked round. This was not the sort of pub she'd ever been to before. It smelt strongly of stale beer, smoke and sweat. The carpets were sticky. Dusty photos of old Wakefield adorned the greasy yellow-stained walls. An old-fashioned jukebox stood in a dark corner. She was relieved to see the place seemed to be empty, apart from two skinny, long-haired youths who were playing pool in a back room. Sitting at the table, she was able to study Tara unobserved. She was leaning nonchalantly against the bar as the barman topped up the pints, looking for all the world as if this was her home turf. Erin tried to analyse what she found so attractive in this girl. Her blonde hair was badly cut, long and messy. She wore her usual uniform of ripped jeans and plaid shirt, but this time had added an ancient leather jacket, the seams worn grey, a rip near the back. It was a seedy kind of look, but at the same time glorious. Erin realised that Tara's power lay in not trying too hard, not giving a damn. She and Laura had spent hours in front of the bathroom mirror earlier that evening, without achieving a quarter of the impact.

'Here you go,' said Tara, turning and placing two glasses on the table. 'Cheers.' She took a long pull of her pint and wiped the froth from her lips with the back of her hand. Erin found the gesture thrillingly masculine. 'Now tell me, what's the deal with you and Laura. Are you two lezzies?'

'What? God, no! We're just best friends.'

'Really? You're always so joined at the hip. Always together. I just wondered…'

'No, we're just really old friends. Since kindergarten, actually.'

'She's holding you back, you know.'

'What do you mean?'

'You're different people. You're a traveller. And Laura's a stayer.'

'What do you mean?' Erin asked again, confused.

'I mean, I think there's more to you. You want to go places, have adventures. Laura's not going anywhere. She's… unimaginative.'

'No, you're wrong, she's great!' Erin was swamped by conflicting emotions. She felt fiercely protective of her oldest friend, but a little seed of doubt had been planted. Was Laura stopping her from being who she could be? Holding her back? 'You just don't know her very well yet. She's amazing.'

Tara shrugged. 'If you say so. It's difficult to break old habits. They're comfortable. You've known her forever. But sometimes you have to break away to grow. Just saying… So anyway, what about you? Tell me everything. You go to the High School don't you? What are you doing there? What do you want to do afterwards?'

'I'm doing languages and geography at A-level. I want to travel afterwards. Maybe work in tourism. Tour operator maybe, or work at the airport. What about you, which school do you go to?'

'I don't. I left school this year. I do this and that. I help my mum in her shop sometimes.'

'Really?' Erin was shocked and a little disappointed. That didn't sound very glamorous. 'What kind of shop?'

'She runs Moonlight, the shop down Kirkgate, do you know it?'

'Yeah. I've been in once.' Erin had been drawn towards the brightly coloured crystals in the window display, and tempted in by a particularly beautiful piece of rose quartz. Once inside she'd felt less comfortable in the dark, strange-smelling interior, looking round the shelves packed with ritual oils, herbs, tarot cards, candles, what looked like animal bones and books on every subject connected to spiritualism and the occult. She had hurried out again without a purchase.

'So is your mum a pagan too?'

'Nah. She's a witch.'

'God, so's mine!' They looked at each other for a second, then both snorted with laughter, and Erin began to relax. 'Mine's so controlling. Always wants to know what I'm up to. What time I'll get home, have I done my homework, what marks did I get. My dad's a bit better. He acts as referee between me and Mum when there's an argument. We argue quite a lot. Well, it's not really arguing, it's more like sniping and sulking. Poor old Dad; he gets stuck in the middle all the time. What about your dad? What's he like?' she asked.

'I never knew him. It's always been just me and my mum. But that's OK. We get along fine. Want another beer?'

Erin was shocked to see Tara had finished her pint already. Jesus, she thought, she drinks like a man! 'No, we'd better go now. At least try and get some of the items. Look, here's a start.' She picked up the nearest beer mat and stuffed it in her bag.

'And this makes two,' said Tara, leaning across to pick up an empty crisp packet that had been rolled up, knotted and stuffed inside a glass on a nearby table. 'I've got purple knickers on; I'll take them off in the loo later.' Then she stood up and shouted towards the two lads in the back room: 'Oi! Either of you two got a bus ticket on you, by any chance? It's for a stupid fucking scavenger hunt.'

One of the boys paused, fished into the pocket of his denim jacket and did find a bus ticket. He sauntered over with a leering smile and waggled it between his thumb and forefinger.

'Swap it for a kiss?'

'In your dreams, arsehole! But ta very much.' Tara snatched the ticket and dismissed the boy with a wave of her hand. 'You can fuck off back to your game now.'

Erin gawped. What enviable panache! What perfectly pitched breezy confidence. She's not intimidated by the opposite sex at all. Quite the opposite. Will I ever be able to swear at a stranger, she thought, at a boy? How liberating that must be.

'That's four things,' said Tara, sitting back down. 'I know where there's a road sign we can nick on the way back. That'll do, easy, sorted. So, you got any money on you, or do I have to get the next round in as well?'

***

Laura was strangely subdued on the drive home. Erin waited until Simon had pulled away from the curb with a wave before asking:

'Are you OK? Did you have a good time tonight? Did you talk to Hamza?'

Laura shrugged. 'Yeah, it was fun. He's really nice and we came second.' She gave Erin a sideways glance. 'You didn't get many things, though, did you? Not even the easy stuff like the stone. What did you and Tara do all night?'

'Well, we ended up just talking for most of the night. She wasn't bothered about winning at all.'

'No,' breathed Laura. 'I think she's playing a different game. One that she does want to win.'

'What do you mean?' asked Erin, for the third time that night.

'Oh, nothing. It doesn't matter. Let's go in. I'm tired.'

***

Over the next few weeks, the cracks widened. Laura sensed that Tara was out to get her, but it was oh so subtle. So innocent. Erin seemed completely unaware of what was happening.

'Oh, your hair looks lovely tonight!' Tara would say to her with a sweet smile, and then give an almost imperceptible snort that only Laura could hear.

When the group were gathered together in the field, ready for an outdoor game, Tara would somehow manage to insert herself in front of Laura, blocking her view of the others, effectively excluding her. Was it deliberate? Only Laura seemed to think so.

When Laura opened her mouth to add to the conversation at the end of a session, Tara would coincidentally speak at the same time, and effortlessly divert everyone's attention to herself.

'Oh, I'll do that for you!' Tara offered one evening, when it was a craft night and Laura was charged with some fiddly gluing. 'I know you're left-handed and a bit clumsy. Oh, sorry, I didn't mean to offend you, but I couldn't help noticing. Give it here.' Again that sickly false smile.

Don't go red, don't go red, Laura told herself. Stay calm! Don't react. Laugh it off.

Then gradually things became a little worse.

'Your label's sticking out of your jumper, honey. Here, let me just tuck it in for you.' As Tara reached out sharp, black-nailed fingertips towards her neck, Laura shivered with sudden revulsion.

'No, just fuck off, will you?' she exploded, and everyone stopped what they were doing and stared, shocked.

Laura looked at their stunned faces and felt tears come into her eyes. She rushed out of the room and down the corridor towards the toilets before the tears could fall.

'It must be the wrong time of the month,' she heard Tara say before the door swung shut. 'Poor thing. I'm sure she didn't mean it. She's really touchy though, isn't she?'

'Are you OK, Laura?' asked Erin, joining her in the toilets as Laura splashed water on her flaming cheeks.

'Not really. Tara's got it in for me. She's trying to exclude me. Can't you see?'

'Um, no, not really. What did she do? I mean, what else has she done?'

'Oh, she talks over me, she goes to sit next to me, then changes her mind, she gives me these superior looks when no-one is watching...'

'Are you sure you're not imagining it? I haven't noticed anything in particular.'

'I am not imagining it. She's trying to come between us. Between me and the others too.'

'I don't think... Anyway, don't worry, Laura, nothing can come between us. You're my oldest friend! My best friend. Come back into the room and we'll sit together.'

***

Then, on her seventh week in the group, Tara ramped things up a notch.

The quiz had finished, and they had started to stack the

chairs, wash up the tea mugs, put the papers in the bin and make sure the room was left as they'd found it. But Tara had other plans.

'Right,' she said. 'Sod this. Who's coming to the pub?'

'No-one,' snapped Fiona. 'We haven't finished clearing up.'

'Oh, sod the cleaning. It looks OK to me. Tom? Are you coming?'

Like a faithful puppy, Tom gave Fiona an apologetic shrug, threw his tea towel onto a chair and walked towards the door. 'OK,' he said. 'Sounds fun.'

'OK. Cool. Hamza, I guess you don't drink, do you? Bob? No? Erin? Coming?'

Erin hesitated, caught between conflicting emotions. This was the moment of truth. The time to plant her flag. To make a decision. Am I going to be nice, reliable but boring, or cool, interesting and selfish? Where do I belong? Slowly, Erin leant the broom she was holding against the wall. 'Um...I...' she hesitated. She was aware of Laura staring at her.

'What about me?' whined Millie.

'Sorry, sweet pea. I don't think they'd let you in,' said Tara, quite kindly. 'You're still a bit too young. But I'll see you next week. I've got something special for you. Erin, are you coming, or what?'

Erin looked at Fiona, then at Laura, who was shaking her head, arms folded, confident her friend would refuse. 'Sorry,' she muttered, then broke eye contact and slowly went to fetch her bag.

'No! Wait, wait a minute!' Laura jumped up and held out a hand. 'What the fuck...You can't just leave everything else to us, it's not fair. Erin! Don't go!'

'Sorry,' said Erin again, 'I'll see you back at the house.'

'Wait, think! How will you get home? You'll have to walk. It's dangerous walking through the underpass at night.'

'She'll be OK,' said Tara. 'She's not a baby. Come on. Let's go.'

With that, they left the room. Millie had started crying and

Karen put a comforting arm round her. Laura felt her own eyes stinging with tears. She could feel Simon's sympathetic gaze and knew that one kind word would let her emotions spill over.

'Right then,' she said decisively, leaning down to pick up the tea towel. 'Looks like it's just us. Let's get this place cleaned up.' Serves her right if she gets attacked in the underpass, she thought, dashing away a tear. Serves her bloody well right!

***

Erin fiddled clumsily with the catch, pushed the gate open with her knee and staggered unsteadily towards her front door. Three pints of beer was much more than she was used to; she was drunk. Her head span and her limbs were not behaving. But at least the drink had given her the courage to walk through the stinking underpass without a care. Then she gave a start.

'Fuck! What are you sitting there for?'

Laura stood up from the doorstep slowly and looked at her friend with a stony expression.

'I'm locked out. Your parents went to bed early and you've got the only key. I've been waiting for you to get home.'

'Oh, God, I'm sorry! Fuck! I didn't think.'

'No. You didn't,' Laura continued. 'You just rushed off with your new best friend. Did you have a good time at least?'

'Yeah, it was quite cool, I suppose.' Erin shrugged. She didn't meet Laura's gaze but slid her eyes off to the side.

'What? Not that great? Well, serves you bloody well right for deserting us.'

'It was OK. We played pool and darts and put lots of stuff on the jukebox. That was nice. Yeah it was fun. But... but... Tara kissed Tom.'

'Really?' Laura's voice changed instantly and she took a step towards her friend. 'Oh, Erin, I'm sorry. What a bitch!' She was sympathetic, but also secretly pleased that Tara must have gone down a peg or two in Erin's estimation. 'She just has to have everything, doesn't she? And now she's stolen your boyfriend.

Poor you. Were you really jealous?'

'A bit,' Erin admitted.

Laura put an arm round her friend and they walked together through the door and up the stairs, trying to make as little noise as possible.

That night, Laura fell asleep instantly. In the single bed on the opposite side of the room, Erin was wide awake. She examined her feelings. Yes, she was jealous. Very jealous.

As she'd watched the two blonde heads coming together, witnessed the sensuous way in which Tara looped a hand round the back of Tom's neck to pull him close, she'd felt awkward, excluded and, yes, overcome with jealousy. But not of Tara. Of Tom. What the hell did that mean?

***

'What time did you two get home last night?' asked Erin's mum over breakfast the next morning. 'I didn't hear you come in.'

'Oh, not too late,' lied Erin, with a quick guilty glance at Laura. 'About ten thirty, I think.' She stirred her spoon around the cornflakes bowl but felt too hungover to eat. The sound of Cathy noisily chewing her own breakfast with an open mouth made her feel nauseous.

'Is that nice boy still driving you home? What's his name again?'

'Simon. Yes, don't worry. He says he'll always give us a lift.'

'We should maybe give him a bit of petrol money. Remind me next week and I'll give you a fiver. What's the matter, Erin? You're not eating. Are you not hungry? You look a bit peaky.'

'I don't feel that great actually. I didn't sleep well. I'll walk Laura back to the bus station in a minute. The fresh air will do me good.'

Then Erin remembered something.

'Oh Mum, by the way, there's a first camping trip being

organised for the bank holiday weekend. It's next month, the end of May. We're all planning on going to Malham and doing lots of hiking. Can I go? Please, please? I promise I'll get all my school work done beforehand.'

'Well, I'm not sure about that. And you haven't got a tent or a backpack. Or walking boots for that matter. That's all expensive.'

'I can borrow most of what I need, and there's plenty of space in other people's tents already, I don't need my own. Please, Mum.'

'I don't know. I'll have to think about that. What do your parents say, Laura?'

Laura opened her mouth to answer, but Erin jumped in:

'Oh, they're totally cool with it. They've agreed. Everybody else's parents are OK with it. You and Dad are very protective. That's really nice and shows how much you care, but you have to let go a bit. We're sixteen after all. Some people are married at sixteen.'

'Oh, heaven forbid! We'll see. I'll speak to your father. And to Laura's parents. I want to know all the details before I decide.'

***

'Bloody hell, that was a whopping great lie you told your mum!' Laura complained as they waited for the bus to pull in to the parking bay at the bus station. 'What's going to happen when your mum phones mine?'

'Well, I was hoping you'd manage to persuade your parents quickly. Can you ask them straight away, when you get back home? Your parents are quite relaxed aren't they? I'm sure they'll agree to it.'

'You should have asked me before. I hate being trapped in a lie. And you've got a real cheek asking a favour after that stunt you pulled last night. I'm still not really speaking to you.'

'Laura, I'm sorry. I won't let you down again. You're the most important person in the world to me. But can you ask them? Please, please? It'll be amazing to go camping with everyone. No parents, no rules, freedom. Don't you want to?'

Laura hesitated. She didn't want to give in too quickly. She wanted Erin to realise how upset she'd been. But as she looked at Erin's imploring face, she cracked.

'OK, I'll try.'

The bus pulled into the bay at last and stopped with a hiss of brakes. Erin gave her a brilliant smile and a hug.

'You're the best!'

On the half-hour bus journey back to her house, Laura stared out of the window, barely taking in the red-brick semis and neat gardens. She wondered what she'd let herself in for. A three-day weekend. Yes, there'd be freedom and fun. But would Erin be walking beside her, would she share a tent with her, or would she choose Tara? Would she be feeling left out and miserable all weekend? Did she really want to go at all? But she'd promised Erin, now. She couldn't back out.

It'll be OK, she tried to persuade herself. I'm sure it'll be OK. You're being too pessimistic. There's nothing to worry about. It's just a weekend. What's the worst that could happen?

Chapter Seven

Now

This wasn't really working out. She could sense the awkwardness and embarrassment emanating from Ted, even though she could only see him from the corner of her eye. He was hating this. The instructor stood a few metres in front of the class with his back to them, his arms moving fluidly, his hips forming sensual figure-of-eights as he demonstrated the basic steps. It looked so effortless. 'Rhumba', he called out, alternate legs stepping to the side then together in a smooth wave-like motion. Then 'salsa' – and the leg movement changed to forward and back, with a slight eloquent roll of the shoulders. Erin heard Ted swearing and glanced over. He gave a little hop as he attempted to change leg. His face was red and he was sweating profusely. She gave him an encouraging smile but he didn't return it.

Erin had confronted Ted on the previous Sunday evening, asking him to switch off the TV and sit down for a serious talk.

'Ted, you know I've been feeling a bit off for quite a while now,' she began.

'You don't say? I hadn't noticed,' he said with light irony and a soft smile. 'Yeah. You have been a bit out of sorts for a few days.'

'More than that. It's been months. Laura thinks it's to do with turning fifty soon. I feel like time is running out and I'm not making the most of it.'

Ted nodded. 'I think everyone feels a bit like that when a big birthday comes up. I know I didn't like turning forty much. Fifty was better, I didn't mind fifty.'

'I think it's more than that… I just hate being bored. It makes me mean and grumpy, and I don't want to be mean – especially not with you.'

'I can put up with a bit of grumpiness.'

'No, it's not fair on you. And I need to feel better about life.'

'Well, what do you want to do about it? What can we do to cheer you up?'

'Laura suggested joining a sky diving or parachuting club.'

'Ha! Good old Laura. You didn't take her seriously, I hope?'

'No, but I do think it would be good if we did an activity together. Something different to wake us both up a bit.'

'What, both of us? You know I just like to chill out after work. I'm usually knackered. I can't really be arsed going out again in the evenings.' Ted was a recruitment consultant, which was a surprisingly stressful job, especially in the unsure economic climate of the day. He liked his job, but worked long hours and was under constant pressure to meet his targets.

Erin let out a sigh. Be kind, don't get cross, she told herself. 'Would you do it just for me?'

'Well, you're the one who wants cheering up, not me. Oh God… I suppose. It depends. What did you have in mind? Are you thinking something creative, or intellectual, or physical?'

'Maybe something physical? And social? Can we have a look on the internet now and see what's going on? We can maybe find something that suits us both?' She reached for her laptop.

'Go on, then.' Reluctantly he joined Erin on the sofa as she began to scroll down the lists of activities in the surrounding area.

'What about that one there?' asked Ted. 'Environmental Action? That might be fun. Cleaning rubbish from the rivers or planting wildflowers. It'd be physical all right.'

'No, it'll be full of goody-goody ecology bores. Ugh! What else do you like the look of?'

'Um, chess club, or model-making sound OK.'

'Oh Ted! They'll be full of retired people! I don't want to end up feeling even older.'

'Well, what would you go for, then?'

'Archery?'

'No, I tried that once. It knackers the inside of your elbow. And the gear's expensive.'

'Dance, then.'

'You know I can't dance.'

'Oh, anyone can learn to dance. Look, there's rock or tango or salsa, all on different nights.'

'Nope. No way.'

The conversation had ended without agreement, but Erin hadn't given up. Over the next few nights she hinted, wheedled and cajoled, until at last Ted had capitulated. On the Thursday evening he had driven them both to the salsa class with the expression of someone being led to the gallows. While Erin made a few bland opening remarks to the other students he had skulked at the back of the gym, his hands in his pockets.

Now here he was, desperately out of his comfort zone and hating every minute.

'OK. Find your partner and now practice these steps together,' called the instructor. 'Obviously if the man steps forward with the right, the woman steps back with the left. If the man steps to the left, the woman steps to the right. Off you go!'

Erin took one of Ted's sweaty hands in hers and placed his other hand on her shoulder. Together they shuffled pitifully about the room, heads down, looking at their feet.

'Ow!'

'Dammit, sorry.'

'It's OK. You're doing great.'

'Please don't patronise,' said Ted, through gritted teeth.

At last the hour was up. They made their way silently to the car park. Once inside the car, Ted let out a long breath.

'Thank God that's over,' he said.

'It was just the first one. It wasn't so bad. It'll get better. You will come again next week won't you?'

'No. That was humiliating. I felt like a complete plonker. It's not for me. I tried it, you can't say fairer than that. But sorry, love, I don't think I'll be going back there again.'

'Ted! You can't give up after one go!'

'Look, I tried it. I didn't like it. End of.'

'But…'

'Just leave it, can't you? I said no,' said Ted, with unaccustomed firmness.

Erin fumed silently on the short drive home. They hung up their coats and took off their shoes in silence. Ted lined his shoes up neatly by the door and searched for his slippers. Then he turned towards the stairs.

'Are you coming to bed?' he asked.

'Not yet. I'm still too keyed up.' Erin replied, tersely.

She expected Ted to respond to this, to apologise, to offer to talk or give her a hug, but instead he just shrugged and made his way up to the bedroom. The way his slippered feet scuffed on the stairs annoyed her. His slippers themselves suddenly made her feel furious – those disgusting old-man tartan slippers. He would wear them all day if he could. She heard him in the bathroom carefully brushing his teeth and that annoyed her too. Christ! she thought. He didn't even give it a chance tonight. Are we really suited? Were we ever? How come we've got to this stage in our marriage and I'm just realising I married a… a… couch potato! But he wasn't always like this, was he? She pictured the years ahead, rolling away in a haze of TV-watching inertia. Slippers and television. Fuck that.

She'd met Ted relatively late, when she was twenty-seven and he was thirty, at a mutual friend's birthday party. Erin hadn't intended to go; she was tired after work, but had a last-minute change of mind, threw on some clean jeans, retrieved her favourite top from the laundry basket and headed into town. She'd arrived close to ten o'clock, when most of the guests were pleasantly drunk, talking loudly and dancing with abandon. Erin couldn't catch up, and felt at a loss, wishing she hadn't come. She clung to the wall, drink in hand, wondering if anyone would notice if she left. Then she caught sight of the lanky, brown-haired man sitting on the sofa in the corner of the living room, leafing through the host's LP collection. He looked serious, intelligent – and sober. He picked up an album and pored over the cover, then replaced it. She went over to join him. 'Find anything good?' she asked. 'Depends on your taste,' he'd replied, and a conversation about music started. She found him easy to talk to, quite without artifice or conceit. By the end of the night they had exchanged phone numbers and planned to meet for coffee at the weekend. Erin liked his earnestness, his respect, the way he didn't rush anything or push too hard. He hadn't tried to kiss her when they said goodnight, but the warmth in his eyes when he smiled at her had been sexy. Over the next month they began to date, with trips to the cinema or to the restaurant. Erin liked his measured, unflappable nature. It was in stark contrast to her previous boyfriends. She had a string of failed relationships behind her, with men who had been exciting, but unreliable and mercurial. She'd thrown herself into each one with reckless abandon, but maybe it was time for a change. The women's magazines she occasionally read in doctors' waiting rooms often suggested you should try dating someone completely outside your usual type. Well, this man couldn't be more different. She'd give it a go. Six months later, they got engaged. Her nickname for him was 'My Steady Ed.' Her parents loved him.

The marriage was perfect to begin with; their different characters complemented each other well. He'd always been on an even keel emotionally, while her moods swung back and forth constantly. But physically he'd been fit and active back then. If Erin was the one who had a sudden urge to throw clothes into a bag and head off to the coast if the weekend weather forecast was good, then Ted was more than willing to jump into action with the practicalities. He would be the one to fill up the car, to root out the walking gear, to book the accommodation. He had curiosity, too; he would look in the newspaper, pondering over the 'what's on this week' section, and persuade her to go along to strange art exhibitions or world-music concerts. He'd been a patient but energetic father, spending hours in front of a football net when Matt went through his football phase. He would go cycling for miles with Beth.

When had he started to change? she asked herself now. And why? Was it just the pressure of his work? Was he going to rediscover his drive when he retired, or was it always going to be like this? He was heavier now, could do with losing a stone or two. Would that make a difference to his energy levels? She thought of the article she'd read in the Daily Express yesterday. It said that after the age of twenty-five, your brain gets lazy. You get stuck in a rut, your neurones don't fire properly. If you're not careful, your brain cells start to die off, you lose the ability to make leaps of imagination, to think creatively. The article recommended any kind of new hobby – a language, an instrument, chess, a sport – anything to get the brain cells firing up again. She'd shown the article to Ted, saying 'Look! It's brilliant we're going to salsa tomorrow; it says here that a new hobby can actually give you benefits in your work life too; you'll open up new neural pathways and become more strategic.' Ted had just grunted non-committally.

Tonight had been a disaster, but she would not give in. Fuck it! she thought. I will not live like that. If Ted isn't going to change, I'll do it on my own. Our time on this earth is precious, limited. God only knows what's round the corner. This year two friends my age have found out they have cancer. I will not waste my time!

Instead of climbing the stairs, she reached for her phone and checked her emails. She looked at WhatsApp and replied to a couple of comments. Then she clicked on the Facebook icon. She saw it immediately and her heart gave a little jump. There hadn't been any reaction to her Facebook searches for weeks, she'd almost forgotten about them, but now here it was: one new friend request accepted. She looked at the photo. Was that really…? Could it really be the same person? He looked so different. He looked really good! Memories flooded back. Wow! When had she seen him for the last time? Had he attended the funeral? Erin thought not. So the last time would have been… that weekend. That camping trip to the Dales. The weekend she'd almost completely blocked from her mind.

Nine people had set off with light hearts, heavy backpacks and high hopes that weekend, but one of them had never returned. No-one knew for sure how it had happened. They had been questioned over and over again by the police, and again at the inquest but it had remained a mystery. A verdict of accidental death had been recorded by the coroner. It was something Erin chose not to dwell on, herself. Why focus on the bad stuff? Anyway, it was all in the past wasn't it, surely? Ages ago. They were all over it now, weren't they? What harm could it do to get back in contact?

Erin was wrong. Most of the old group had put the death behind them, but for one person it was far from over.

Sometimes one death can lead to another.

Chapter Eight
Three weeks until the accident

Laura tried to ignore the blister on her heel as she trudged along the footpath. She was wearing her Dad's old walking boots, freshly daubed with a layer of dubbin, and they were rubbing terribly despite the two pairs of socks. Her brother's backpack was comfortable enough, but it was old fashioned, more of an army surplus knapsack. The light drizzle was bound to seep through the canvas, making it even heavier. She looked up at Erin, walking just ahead on the narrow path. She must have managed to persuade her dad to buy not only a modern lightweight nylon backpack, but also a sturdy pair of padded boots. She wondered how that had gone down with Erin's more frugal mum. At least they didn't have to carry the tents; that was the boys' job. The group had decided to do the short walk to Emley Moor on this dull Saturday morning, in order to test their gear before the big camping weekend.

Tara was not with them today, and for that, Laura was grateful. The very presence of Tara made her feel on edge, scared even. The others couldn't seem to see that, and Laura wondered why. Millie was completely in thrall to her, hanging on her every word. Fiona seemed strangely cowed by her, becoming submissive, unable to assert her authority as she normally did. The boys were obviously attracted to her; she was undoubtedly sexy, with her flashing green eyes and her just-out-of-bed messy blonde hair. Karen and Simon seemed to accept her well enough, and as for Erin, well, all she saw, all she really chose to see, was the confidence, the devil-may-care coolness. She looked no further than that. Why am I the only one that senses the cruelty that lies beneath? Laura pondered. I wonder what makes Tara the way she is? Does she need to play with people's emotions to make herself feel better? Is her home life awful? Maybe she needs to control people because she has no control over her own life. But that was not really an excuse.

Even though Tara had not joined them on the walk today, Laura still did not feel at ease. Something was wrong. She could no longer seem to find the easy camaraderie with the other group members. When she'd walked next to Simon as they'd crossed the field just now, the conversation had seemed stilted, and he'd given her a strange look. Embarrassed, or maybe pitying? Questioning? She couldn't quite put her finger on it. Millie kept glancing over at her too, as if she was trying to work something out. She had the horrible feeling that Karen and Fiona, way ahead, were talking about her behind her back.

No, I'm imagining things, she chided herself. I'm feeling a bit left out of things because of school. These are my friends, my true friends.

School had become difficult of late. Laura knew she wasn't part of the cool clique, but it had never bothered her before. She had her group of friends; Erin of course, and Sophie, Alison, Mary. They were quiet, studious, self-effacing, but supportive. The same little knot of friends had been together for years now. But lately she felt that Erin was pulling away. She looked different; she was looping her tie round and round the knot to make it fatter. She was rolling her skirt around the waistband to shorten it. She'd bought shoes with a platform heel, even though this was not permitted. Her nails were polished with clear varnish and she wore her mascara to school – again against the rules. More and more often she'd say to Laura 'Come on, let's go talk to Jacqui and Harriet.' Or 'Let's eat lunch at that table with Sally and Isobel for a change.' And she'd pull Laura along in her wake to where the ice-queens of the class were sitting. These were the cream, the elite. The girls with identical flicked-back fringes and cool stares. Laura watched as these girls assessed Erin's appearance and her suitability to join their clique. They invited her to sit, they made conversation, but Laura knew it was a kind of probation. They didn't address a single word to Laura herself.

I'm losing Erin, I'm losing her, she thought. I'm not enough for her. How do I stop this? Do I try to go with her, or retreat back to my safe place? Do I just accept it?

And now she had a similar feeling within the group. What was happening? Is there something wrong with me? Have I done something wrong?

After an hour's steady climb, the group paused by a stone wall under the towering TV mast, shrugged off their backpacks and unpacked sandwiches with numb fingers. The drizzle had become steady rain now, and they hunched inside their anoraks as they ate.

'I hope the weather's not like this in Malham,' said Laura. 'It'll be horrible trying to put up the tents.'

There was a murmur of agreement, but nothing more. Laura tried again:

'I like your walking boots, Hamza. Where did you get them?'

'Oh, thanks. Millets, in town.' But Hamza didn't quite meet her eye as he answered, and there the conversation died. This is not normal, thought Laura. What is going on?

It wasn't until they were making their way back down towards the starting point that Laura found out what the problem was. Millie was trotting along next to her, glancing across at her frequently with a puzzled expression.

'What's up?' asked Laura. 'Is something wrong?'

'No, not really. I just wanted to ask you. Is it true?'

'Is what true?'

'What the others are saying?'

'What are they saying?'

'You know, the thing at school.'

'What are you talking about? What thing? What are they saying?' Laura asked again.

'Um... That you fell in love with a maths teacher at your school and started stalking him and sending him love letters and stuff, and he had to resign.'

'What? What on earth are you talking about? Who told you that?'

'Everyone's talking about it.'

'Of course it's not true. Of course not! Where did you get this from? Who told you?'

'I don't know. It's just what everyone's saying. I heard Karen saying to Fiona.'

'Oh my God! There is absolutely no truth in this. It's a horrible rumour. I bet Tara started it.'

'No, I don't think so. She's not here today anyway, so she couldn't have.'

'Listen, you tell the others it's a load of absolute nonsense. Jesus! I can't believe this! Just ask Erin. She'll tell you what a load of bollocks this is. Erin! Come here! I need you.'

Erin turned, walked back to them and said: 'What's up? You look terrible. What's the matter?'

Laura could hardly speak. 'It's... oh fuck... there's a disgusting rumour going round about me. Oh God! They're all saying it was me that stalked that maths teacher at school and made him resign.'

Erin burst out laughing. 'What? That's ridiculous. You're the last person on earth to stalk a teacher.'

'It's not funny, Erin! It's damaging. They've all got this weird impression of me now.'

'Don't worry about it. I bet they're all secretly impressed as hell.'

'No! You don't get it, do you? This is not me. This is... oh shit.

Character assassination. It's Tara. I bet she started it.'

'Laura, look, don't worry. I'll tell everyone it's not true. I don't know how these things start, but I doubt it was Tara. She doesn't know anything about our school. Laura, don't cry, it's not the end of the world. These things blow over so quickly. I'll talk to everyone now.'

Erin was as good as her word. As they waited for the bus back to town, she went to each person in turn, assuring them that the rumours were false. There had been a young maths teacher who had left last year, but that had absolutely nothing to do with Laura. She hadn't even been in his maths class.

'There. Sorted.' she said, coming to stand next to Laura again. 'I've put them all straight.'

'Do you think they believe you?'

'Of course they do. They know you. They know what you're like. They're your friends. Of course they believe me.'

'What about Tara? I'm sure she's behind this.'

Erin sighed. 'Look, I'll ask her what she knows about it tomorrow.'

'Tomorrow? Sunday? You're seeing Tara tomorrow?'

'Um… yes.' Erin had the grace to look uncomfortable. 'She offered to take me out on her motorbike. We're going onto the moors.'

Laura nodded slowly. 'Of course you are.' She looked away quickly before Erin could see the tears welling once more in her eyes.

***

'What have we stopped here for?' asked Erin. The heather-covered moorland looked bleak and desolate.

They had ridden out through the industrial towns of West Yorkshire, skirting Bradford and riding on through the picturesque town of Haworth. Erin had expected them to stop there and explore the steep cobbled streets and the Bronte parsonage, but instead they had continued onto the rugged moors to the north-west. It was Erin's first time on a motorbike and she found it exhilarating. She kept her arms firmly around Tara's waist as they flew up the single-track roads. The first few corners had been unnerving, and she'd fought to keep upright as Tara leaned into each bend, but gradually she learned to relax and make her body follow the same angle as Tara's. The sense of freedom was intoxicating. But now they had pulled into a scrappy looking parking area, just big enough for two cars. Erin dismounted with some difficulty, pulled off her crash helmet and looked around, expectantly. There was nothing here. The moors stretched in every direction, bleak and barren, broken only by dry stone walls and the occasional sheep.

'It's a special place. My secret place,' said Tara. 'Follow me.'

Tara placed her helmet on the bike seat and headed off into the heather, and Erin rushed to follow. It was tough going. The heather roots snagged at their ankles and the wet earth sucked at their boots. They frequently leapt over oily black bogs. Looking up, Erin became aware of a dark shape up ahead. It appeared at first insignificant, but as they approached it seemed to loom larger and larger. The sky behind it was ever-changing; first blue, then grey, then black, then golden as the wind chased the clouds away from the sun. At last they were standing in front of the massive boulder. It was as tall as a house, its face cut with deep vertical and horizontal fissures. About halfway up, a small, rectangular hole had been cut into the rock face, just large enough for a body to fit into.

'Come on. This is the Hitching Stone. And that hole is the Druid's Chair. Let's climb up and go inside.'

They scrambled up the sheer rock face and squeezed into the small chamber. It was dark inside. Strange symbols had been carved into the walls and roof. Behind them, a curious narrow tunnel led all the way to the other side of the rock, letting in a thin round beam of daylight. It gave the effect of an eye, staring steadily at them.

'Go on, sit down. Can you feel it?'

'Feel what?' Erin lowered herself gingerly onto the rock floor at the entrance of the Druid's Chair. She drew her knees up to her chin and wrapped her arms around them, protectively.

'The energy. The power of the stone. This is a sacred place. A place of pagan worship. People would sit up here at the equinox and watch the sun coming up over Pendle Hill. Listen!'

As the wind whipped around and through the boulder, it seemed to emit a weird, deep humming noise.

'What the hell's that? Where's it coming from?' asked Erin, feeling the first prick of fear.

'It's coming from the stones themselves. They're magic. They're feeling you.' Tara shuffled into the narrow space beside Erin, her body pressed up close behind her. She put one hand on Erin's shoulder and pointed outside.

'That's Pendle Hill. Have you heard of it?'

'No, should I have?'

'The Pendle witch trials? This place has always been a source of magic. Witches have lived here forever. The first ones were healers really. They used their knowledge of herbs to cure illnesses. People respected them and admired them. They paid them a lot of money for their remedies. But then the Catholic church said it was heresy, and witches began to be seen as evil, dangerous, corrupting. They were persecuted, accused of all sorts of rubbish, like killing animals, putting spells on people, cannibalism. They put ten witches to death up there on Pendle Hill.'

'How did they kill them?'

'They hanged them.'

Erin shivered. This place was giving her goosebumps. She couldn't decide whether it was fear or excitement. Somewhere between the two.

'Come on,' said Tara, 'I want to show you something else.'

They left the chamber again and walked around to the side of the oblong boulder. Here the face was less steep and criss-crossed with striations. Very carefully they climbed to the top of the giant rock. A second strange sight caused Erin to gasp. At the top of the boulder was a hole, about eight feet long, with steep vertical sides. It contained a deep pool of water. As they watched, the water lapped gently against the sides, stirred by the wind.

'They say this pool never dries up,' said Tara, reverently. 'It's sacred water. Here! Drink!' She reached down to scoop a handful of water in her cupped palm and drank, but Erin shook her head. Then Tara did something strange. She reached into the water again and let a few drops of liquid fall onto Erin's head.

'Tara, you're freaking me out here. What are you doing?'

'I'm anointing you. You're in my coven now.' She grinned. 'Just kidding. Don't look so scared.'

They climbed slowly down to the chamber again and looked out over the moors.

'So you really are a pagan?' asked Erin.

'Yes, I am.'

'What does that mean? What do you believe in?'

'Well,' Tara paused. 'I believe in the forces of nature. It's all here if you look around. The rock is the force of the earth. The pool is the force of water. The wind is the force of the air and the sun is the force of fire. All the elements combined. They are life-giving forces and we must honour them. We must keep them safe. We honour trees, animals, nature in general. We are all part of nature.'

'Ok, well that sounds like environmentalism to me, not so very bonkers. I could go with that. What else?'

'Well, we believe that each person must find their own way, and not necessarily follow society's rules. Be independent, be honest with yourself. Be free and do what feels like the right thing for you.'

'That sounds OK too, I guess. So there's nothing creepy about it?'

'Nothing at all.'

'But do you have, like, powers? Can you evoke forces? You said you could read palms. Can you really see the future?'

Tara hesitated. 'Maybe. Sometimes. If I tell you a secret, will you promise not to share it?'

'Yes, of course.'

'My real name isn't Tara. It's Ostara.'

'So...?'

'My mum named me after the Goddess Ostara. She's the goddess of spring and of the dawn. She's responsible for rebirth, renewal, growth, that kind of thing. She is happy and joyful but can also be temperamental and nasty, like the spring weather. And I think that my mum really believes I am her. In reincarnation.'

'But that's crazy!'

'Yep, it is. Pure bat-shit crazy.'

'You don't believe that?'

'Of course not. Mum's just mental. Forget I said anything.'

They climbed carefully down to the base of the rock. Erin looked around. There was almost nothing to see in any direction. Just bare moorland and endless sky.

'However did you find this place? It's so out of the way. I've never even heard of it!'

'I used to live round here.'

'Really? Did you?'

'Yeah. We lived with my Gran. In Silsden.'

'Why did you move to Wakefield?'

'Gran died two years ago. Mum sold the house so she could start up the shop. We moved to the flat on the Eastmoor Estate.'

'Do you miss it here?'

'God, yeah. A lot. My Gran taught me everything I know about the moors, nature, folklore. We'd walk for miles.'

'Was she a pagan?'

'Nah, more what you'd call a wise woman. She could predict the weather and tell you why your hens weren't laying, that kind of thing. She was... ah, she was just...' Tara's voice cracked and

Erin felt a wave of compassion. She put an arm round Tara, but it was shrugged off.

'Come on, let's go.'

'Wait, can I ask you something else?'

'OK. If you must.'

'Why don't you like Laura?'

Tara's eyes flashed briefly at the name. She did not like Laura. Laura made her uncomfortable. She saw through her, was immune to her charm. In truth, Laura threatened her just a little bit. But there were ways of dealing with that.

'She's earth and water. I'm air and fire. We're polar opposites and can't be friends,' she said, breezily.

'And what am I? Air, water, earth or fire?'

'That's what you've got to find out for yourself.'

Erin took a breath. 'Tara, did you start that rumour about Laura? About her stalking a teacher at school?'

'No. I can't remember where I heard it. Someone I met in the pub who went to your school, I think. Why, isn't it true?'

'You know it isn't. She'd never do anything like that. Laura thinks you started it.'

'Laura can think what she likes. I don't give a shit. Come on. Let's go before it rains.'

On the ride back home, Erin mulled over their conversation. She wanted to be air, she wanted to be fire. But deep down she suspected that she was earth, boring old earth, just like Laura.

Tara dropped her off outside her house and Erin made her way up the path to her front door. Then she stopped. Her mother stood in front of the door, arms folded over her chest, her lips pressed into a thin line of disapproval.

'I want a word with you, young lady!' said her mother. 'You told us you were going out for the day with a friend. You did not say anything about a motorbike. You know how your father and I feel about motorbikes. They are deadly. You are not allowed to go on them. And who was that strange girl with the bleached hair?'

All the mixed up emotions of the day came to an explosive head. Erin lost her cool. 'Her name's Tara and she's a pagan!' she shouted, defiantly. 'She believes in making her own rules, and so do I!' She pushed past her mother into the house and ran up the stairs.

'Come back here right now, young lady! You needn't think you're going on that camping trip if you speak to me in that tone of voice again. Come back and apologise.'

Erin threw herself on the bed and yelled into the pillow in frustration. God, what a confusing day! Weird, scary – but kind of exciting too. Paganism. A word she'd always associated with horror films. Erin adored horror films, especially the old seventies ones that came on the TV in the small hours. The Wicker Man was one of her favourites. She'd seen The Witches several times, and the ridiculously named Blood on Satan's Claw was well worth a watch. All these films treated paganism as a dangerous, subversive cult, with a strong sexual undercurrent and a penchant for human sacrifice. But Tara's definition was quite different. It encompassed ecology, respect, self-determination, a sense of one's place within the natural world. All that was very attractive. Very modern, in fact.

Erin had been confirmed at the age of eleven, as was expected. She had gone to church with her family every Sunday when she was younger. She had found the whole thing boring, stifling. She used to sit through the sermons questioning every aspect of what she was being told. We are being asked to believe in something you can't see or prove, and being told that believing without questioning is a sign of great faith. Well stuff that, we should question things. Blind faith is like jumping off a cliff and expecting to land on a soft cushion of flowers. How much more pure, more simple, to believe in the power of nature. The wind, the sea, the rocks. Things that we can witness all around us. Maybe I should be a pagan too. The idea of challenging her parents' expectations and assumptions was alluring.

Erin didn't worry about her mother's threat to cancel the camping trip. Her mum always overreacted initially and then calmed down later. Her bark was much worse than her bite. She would get her father alone tonight and pull him round to her side. There was no way she would miss out on the camping trip.

But everything would have been so different if she had.

Chapter Nine
One week until the accident

It was the last Friday before the camping trip. It was games night and the idea was to bring simple games that people could jump in and out of, so that everyone could try something different in the course of the evening. Monopoly and Diplomacy were definitely off the list. Erin had brought Connect 4, the easiest of games. Laura brought her Mastermind and Tom was bringing a game called Lunacy. Karen said she'd bring something called Bedbugs. Laura and Erin had arrived early, and were helping Fiona set up half a dozen small tables in the assembly hall, with a cluster of chairs around each. Eventually the last group members filed into the room, and Fiona clapped her hands to get everyone's attention.

'OK everyone, before we start, I just want to go over the plans for next weekend.' There was a collective groan, but Fiona took no notice. She started to distribute sheets of paper. 'Right. We meet at the train station at six-thirty on Saturday morning. That's Westgate Station everybody, not Kirkgate.' Someone muttered a weary 'we know!' but Fiona carried on regardless. 'We get the six-forty-five train to Skipton, then change to the bus station and get the bus to Gargrave. From there we walk about six and a half miles following the river Aire – that's quite flat and should be easy – to our campsite on Cross Keys Farm. That should take about two and a half hours, so we should arrive before midday. On Sunday we do the circular walk to Malham, Janet's Foss waterfall, Goredale Scar and Malham Cove – that is about eight miles, a bit more challenging, but we won't have our tents and stuff in the backpacks, so it should be OK. On Monday we can either walk again in the morning, or just hang about at the campsite. We get the bus back from Malham to Skipton around lunchtime. Right. Food. Has everyone got their list? Does everyone know what to bring? Good. So don't forget the little things like torches, matches, sticking plasters, water bottles. Obviously sleeping bags, airbeds if you have the space. Um, who's bringing camping stoves? Tom and Hamza. Good. Check. Tin openers and bottle openers? Laura? Check. Bin bags and tea towels? Karen? Check.' She continued to go through the items on her list, one by one, ticking them off. 'Right, that's it, I think. We've got enough money in the subs tin to pay for the campsite, but everyone has to get their own train and bus tickets. OK? Right! Let's set the games up then.'

The evening started off well. Some of the games were quiet and strategic, some loud and raucous. Every twenty minutes or so, Fiona rang a little bell and they all swapped tables to start something new. Tom was tactical, he wanted to win, but Karen seemed to have luck on her side that night. Millie was over-excited, laughing wildly and frequently knocking play pieces onto the floor. Erin noticed that Tara was sitting out most of the games. Sometimes she would stop to watch, and sometimes she wandered round the edges of the room, seeming bored. But as the evening grew darker, Erin noticed Tara setting something up in a shadowy corner of the hall, away from the main lights. As enthusiasm for the games started to flag, Tara strolled over into the middle of the group, took Fiona's little bell from her unresisting hand and rang it. Fiona protested, annoyed. Everyone else looked round in surprise.

'Right. I've got a game I don't think you'll have played before. Who's up for something new?'

There was a strange gleam in her eyes and Laura was

instantly on the alert.

'What is it?' asked Tom, rising from his chair.

'Come and see. I need at least four players. Who's in?'

They followed her to the other end of the hall. A gold-coloured oblong board lay on the table, with a pear-shaped wooden block lying on top. In the centre of this block a small magnifying glass was embedded, and on the surface of the board were letters of the alphabet, numbers, and the words Yes and No.

'What's this game, then?' asked Millie. 'How do you play?'

'It's a Ouija board isn't it?' breathed Erin. She'd seen this in horror films. Despite her love of horror films she was not at all sure she wanted to experience this in real life.

'You can't bring that in here!' Fiona was horrified. 'It's dangerous. It's asking for trouble!'

'What are you scared of, Fiona? You don't believe in ghosts or spirits do you? I shouldn't think so, if you're a good Christian. So there's nothing to worry about.'

'Get it out of here! I'm not having that in here!'

'Come on, it's just a bit of fun. Who wants to try? Tom?' Of course, Tom sat down eagerly, his expression animated. 'Right two more. Erin?'

'No, I'm not sure. I'll just watch.'

'Simon? Karen?'

To Erin's surprise, Simon and Karen sat at the table with Tom.

'Erin, can you turn some of the lights out?' asked Tara. 'It makes it more fun in the dark.' She sat down at the table and told the others how to put their fingertips on the wooden planchette. Now in semi-darkness, Hamza, Erin, Laura and Millie stood a little distance away from the table as the others began to play. Fiona had withdrawn to the other end of the room in protest.

'Right. It's pretty easy basically. You ask a question and the board answers. Who's got a question?'

'Um... will it rain at the weekend?'

All stared intently at the planchette. It did not move.

'Try another question.'

'Is there anybody there?' asked Tom in an exaggerated spooky voice. Again the planchette remained still.

'Well, this is a bit lame,' said Simon, and just then, the planchette seemed to tremble slightly.

'How many people are in this room?' asked Karen, thinking this was an easy way to tell if the board worked or not. Immediately the planchette shot to the number nine. Three of the players jumped back in their seats and snatched their hands away in shock.

'Who moved it? Who did that?' asked Simon. They looked at each other and shrugged.

'Cool!' said Tom. 'Maybe it's working!'

'You've got to keep your fingers on the planchette,' said Tara. 'Come on! Don't be scared. They say it just works off our collective conscience. There aren't really any spirits in the room. Or maybe there are. Who knows? Who's got another question?'

'Was this school a happy place when it was a school?' asked Simon. The planchette moved slowly to 'No'.

'Does Tara fancy me?' asked Tom, and everyone sniggered.

'Well, you don't need to ask the board that. Obviously I do not,' said Tara, giving Tom a disdainful stare.

And then something strange happened. Without any questions being asked, the planchette began to travel across the board in a series of quick, smooth movements.

'Someone get a pen and paper!' called Tara.

Erin rushed back with paper and began to take down the letters as they were dictated.

'G... E... R... G again - no F, not G... A... L... L again...D...' There was a pause, then it moved again; 'A... N... N... O... T... G... O... G... E... R...' Another pause. 'R... A... L.' Then the planchette shot off the board and fell to the floor.

'Bloody hell!'

'That was cool. Who was moving that? Tara? It was you wasn't it? Very funny!'

But Tara had gone pale. She seemed flustered, just as surprised as the others. 'No,' she said quietly. 'That wasn't me. I didn't move it.'

'What letters have you got, Erin? Let's see,' asked Karen.

'It doesn't make any sense. I didn't get the first few letters. But the first word I've got seems to be 'Gerf' then there's 'alld' and then 'annotgoger', then 'ral'. Could it be another language? German perhaps?' She laid the paper on the table and they examined it.

'It's not German. Swedish perhaps?'

'Does it read anything backwards?'

'No. Still doesn't make sense. What about anagrams? If we unscramble it?'

'It's just rubbish,' said Tara. 'Just random letters. Throw it away, Erin. It's just a silly game.'

Tara looked strangely nervous, and this made Erin feel intrigued. *She knows something! She felt something*, she thought. *Maybe she does have some sort of gift.* Instead of throwing the paper away, she slipped it into her pocket.

'Have you lot finished with that nonsense now?' called Fiona, from the other end of the room. 'Can we stop now? It's nearly quarter to ten. It's clear-up time.' She switched all the lights back on and the mood was immediately broken.

They stacked the chairs and tables back against the walls and put their games back in their bags. Fiona took the metal tin containing the subs from the cupboard in the entrance hall, unlocked it and began to count out the pound coins needed for the campsite. She put them in a pink sequinned purse and tucked that safely away inside her bag.

'OK everyone!' she called. 'Time to lock up. I'll see you all next Saturday morning. Don't be late!'

***

Erin and Laura discussed the events of the night as they got into their pyjamas in Erin's chilly bedroom.

'What did you make of the Ouija board thing?' said Laura. 'Who do you think was moving it? I bet it was Tom.'

'I don't know. At first I thought Tara was moving it, but she seemed genuinely surprised when the letters started coming. She was as freaked out as everyone.' Erin reached for her jeans on the bedroom floor and pulled the crumpled piece of paper out of the pocket. She smoothed it out on the bedside table, under the little lamp. 'Let's look at it again. It's got to mean something. Let's write down all the letters randomly on a notepad and see what we've got.'

It didn't take them long. The letters were not particularly jumbled up; distinct words could be made out, but they were broken into, as if several voices had been speaking at once. Four words jumped out immediately, and sent a delicious tingle of fear through the two girls.

'Bloody hell! Is that just a coincidence?' asked Laura. 'Did we just pull out the words we wanted to see? There are quite a few letters left over that don't fit and that we can't make words out of.'

'I don't know. It could be just that because we're feeling creeped out, our minds are finding creepy words. And you're right, there are lots of letters left over, but that could be because I didn't start taking down the letters at the beginning, so some of the first words are probably missing.'

'But what does it mean? Do you think it could be a warning about the camping trip?'

'It could be anything. But maybe.'

'But a warning for who? For all of us? Do you think we should warn the others? Cancel the trip?'

'God, I don't know. No, it's probably nothing. Like you said, we were just pulling out the words we wanted to see. The trip will be fantastic. Three whole days without our parents breathing down our necks. Real freedom, adventure. We've got to go!'

'I'm not so sure any more. The atmosphere's been a bit weird in the group lately. I was in two minds about going in the first place, but now...' Laura tailed off.

'Come on.' Erin tried to keep her voice bright and positive, unwilling to admit that she too was having doubts. 'We can't let the others down. It'll be great.'

They stared at the notepad until the letters started to blur.
DANGER FALL NOT GO

Neither of them got much sleep that night.

Chapter Ten

Now

'Pub quiz?' suggested Laura, exasperated.

It was a warm, sunny Wednesday afternoon, and the two women had decided to walk around the lake at Newmillerdam, to make the most of a rare synchronized day off. They had followed the gravel path through the shaded woodland, then stopped for a while in a patch of sunshine to throw sticks into the water, trying to entice the elderly cocker spaniel into the lake to cool off. Dudley looked on, bemused, wagging his tail gamely, but was not to be persuaded.

Erin had described the disastrous salsa night, and how frustrated she was still feeling. Ted had been grumpy for a few days after that, but was now trying to find a way back into her good books. He had even booked a weekend away in Northumberland for the October break. Erin complained that this was not enough, and Laura secretly thought: Poor Ted. You don't deserve him! Instead of voicing this thought, she tried to find more solutions.

'Pub quiz,' said Laura again, with more conviction. 'There's one every Friday night at The Star Inn, and Richard's always talked about getting a team together. Salsa was too far out of Ted's comfort zone, but I think he'd like a pub quiz. He's shit-hot on sports trivia, and Richard's good on science. I can do the medical or biology stuff and you can do geography. We'd be the perfect team.'

'Yeah,' said Erin, unenthusiastically. It didn't sound like a rave to her.

'Oh, come on!' said Laura, impatiently. 'You've got to meet him halfway. What do you expect him to do? Completely change character?'

'Yes, maybe. I've got this crazy idea. I thought maybe we could both take a sabbatical. Go to some third world country for a year and help in a school or something. I want to do something radical. A pub quiz is just… is just a sticking plaster on a broken leg.'

'God, Erin, you can't expect him to do that! He loves his job.'

'Yes, more than he loves me, it seems,' replied Erin, unable to keep the bitterness from her voice. 'But think about it; it would be a chance to travel, to learn a new language, to broaden our horizons. To find each other again, maybe. It would be so good for us. And if he doesn't want to do it, well… well I might just do it on my own.'

'What? Erin! You can't do that! Don't be daft. You're thinking about stuff that could break up your marriage! Think about the impact on the children. A year apart? That's madness! Last month you were just talking about doing a new activity. And now you're suddenly talking about going off for a year? Can't you be happy with what you've got? Plus a few smaller changes?'

'No, I'm not like you, I'm… I want more.'

'That's your problem. You always want more.'

Laura looked at her friend critically. She was wearing clothes that a teenager would be happy in: dad-jeans, a three-quarter sleeved black t-shirt, a hooded sweatshirt wrapped around her waist, and clumpy black boots. Her wrists jangled with a collection of beaded bracelets and she'd had a small tattoo inked onto the inside of one wrist. Her hair was carefully coloured with blonde and honey-coloured highlights, and from the back, you could think Erin was eighteen. Only when you looked at her face did you see the tired eyes, the beginning of wrinkles, the make-up that was just a little too thick. Was there more than a hint of desperation in this look? Laura considered her own clothes: practical and comfy stretch jeans, old walking shoes and a faded red t-shirt; She knew her hair was going grey, but quite liked it, thought it would look distinguished when the grey finally replaced the faded auburn. She looked exactly like what she was: a comfortable mum, a late-middle-aged dog walker. And that was fine.

'Erin, don't fight the aging process so much. Embrace it. There's so much to look forward to still. They say the retirement years are the best of all. That's not far away.'

'What, so we can spend even more time at home watching TV?' she said, bitterly. 'No thanks.' She sighed. 'There's so much out there to experience, and we only get one shot at this life.'

'Well, why don't you and Ted sit down and write a bucket list together? You could agree to do, I don't know… maybe one new thing every couple of months.'

'Hmm, maybe. It's an idea. I'm not sure Ted would agree to it. So what would you put on your bucket list?'

'Um… I've never really thought about it, but…go to an opera. Fly in a helicopter. Be part of the audience in a TV show…um… Go to a karaoke club.'

'You've never been to a karaoke club?'

'No, have you?'

'Yes, with work, a couple of times. You should go, it's fun. But Laura, we're different. My bucket list would be completely different. Swim with a shark, jump out of an aeroplane, snowmobile on a glacier, hike the Inca trail. Ted would never go for any of those.'

'But what's brought on this sudden wanderlust?'

Erin paused. She gave a guilty sideways glance to Laura before she answered: 'I know you said not to try and find any of the old gang, not to open up old wounds, but I found Simon recently on Facebook. And we Skyped last week.'

'Simon? Simon Holden? Really?'

'Yeah, and it was a revelation!' Erin became more and more

animated as she described their old friend. 'Oh, Laura, you would not believe it. He's changed so much! He's lost all the weight, he's really quite fit now. Quite, you know, sexy. He lives in London with a girlfriend who's a model, and he's got the coolest job; he's a travel photographer!'

'What the...? He never even had a camera back then, did he?'

'I don't think so. He did a photography course when his mum died. Found out he was really good at it. He worked two or three jobs for money and took photos in his spare time. Then he got some work for some local papers, won some competitions, went freelance – and now he travels all over the word and gets paid a fortune.'

'Bloody hell! Simon! That is really cool. I'm so glad for him. So... you had quite a chat with him?'

'Yes. And yes, you're right, it made me even more restless. I'm happy for him, but I'm jealous as hell of his lifestyle.'

'Did you talk about the old days? About the accident?'

'No.'

'Good. Has he been in contact with anyone else from back then?'

'No. Oh, just Millie, very briefly. He came back up to Wakefield to give a talk at his old school – you know, careers advice, a former pupil who made it big, blah, blah, blah... And he ran into Millie at the train station. She was working in the coffee shop there, washing up.'

'Millie? Was she? God, what a nutcase she was. She must still live around here then. I've been into that coffee shop loads of times; I've never seen her there. Did he say how she was doing?'

'No, not really. But she told him she wanted to find me again, for some reason. She gave him her mum's phone number, and Simon asked if I wanted him to pass my number on to her mum.'

'What did you say?'

'Well, I didn't see why not. I said yeah, sure.'

'Erin, you're daft. You're chasing after memories that weren't all that good in the first place. Yes, Simon was great, but Millie was really flaky. Especially that last weekend. She was all over the place.'

'She was only fourteen at the time. Yeah, she was a nutter. But she's an adult now, probably married with kids. I don't know what you're so worried about.'

'Do me a favour. Don't arrange to meet her. Or Simon. Let it go.'

'Well... she probably won't ring anyway. And I haven't arranged anything else with Simon. But aren't you just a bit curious?'

'No. Let sleeping dogs lie. Don't go digging up the past.'

'OK,' Erin said, a little too carelessly. 'Come on, let's go round the lake again, then go to the Boathouse Café for a snack. You can take dogs in there, and we can sit on the decking in the sun.'

'OK. But no more talk about the old days. Deal?'

'Deal.'

***

It was a hollow promise. Don't go digging up the past, Laura had said. But for Erin it had become an addiction, and obsession. Her thoughts went back time and time again to those heady first days of adolescent freedom, the excitement, the sense of community, the laughter. Oh, to feel so alive, so in the moment!

On impulse, she ignored the turn-off to Sandal, where her sensible, sterile, modern home was waiting for her, but instead continued straight on into the centre of Wakefield. She drove past the retail outlets and the fast food joints. Everything had changed since she was a girl. New dual carriageways cut through the old neighbourhoods, leaving odd, truncated cul-de-sacs. High-rise flats had been built, but looked empty of life. The stately old Victorian buildings now looked out of place next to the new. It was a jumble, a mess. Where was it? How did you get to the road back then? Eventually she found the street she was looking for. She parked the car in the little parking area, just as her father had done so many years before, and walked down the road towards the old school. She remembered how excited she and Laura used to feel as they approached the building. She felt a similar little flutter of anticipation now.

She stopped and stared. It was a scene of desolation, of destruction. The stone wall had gone. In its place stood a high metal fence with a sign marked 'Danger. Demolition in progress. Do not enter.' She saw two mechanical diggers and several enormous blue skips in what had once been the playground. The left-hand part of the building, where the smaller classrooms had once been, was gone, leaving a giant pile of rubble and broken timbers. The windowpanes in what was left of the building were smashed and the doors boarded up. Erin read the sign again. A new retail park was being constructed here. The once fine Victorian architecture was soon to be replaced by bland, generic shop fronts and a bare expanse of car park. Just what the city needs, though Erin, sourly, another retail park. The current ones don't even get enough footfall.

As she stood behind the metal fence, her mind began to play tricks. She imagined she could hear laughter coming from the field behind the school. Just for a moment, she thought she could see a face in the window of what had been the assembly hall. She could smell again that special school smell – a mixture of ink, dust and cleaning fluids. She shut her eyes for a moment, and the building re-emerged as it once had been; shabby, streaked with pollution, but proud, friendly – welcoming. She saw Tara leaning against the wall, Hamza and Tom play-fighting in the yard and herself – yes, her younger self, walking up the path towards the door. A deep yearning gripped her and she swayed slightly, steadying herself with one hand on the metal fence.

They had been good days, so, so good. People say that your schooldays are the best days of your life, but Erin hadn't particularly enjoyed school. School hadn't formed her, it had just educated her. No, those Friday evenings spent here in this shabby old building with the eclectic group of friends had been the high spot, her heyday. The time when she'd felt the most alive, the most vibrant version of herself. She realised that she'd been searching to regain that feeling for a long, long time.

Erin sighed and blinked. The building returned to dust and rubble once more. Depressed, she walked slowly down the street, back to her car. Nostalgia had her in its grip and she gave in to it totally. She decided to drive the short distance north and parked outside the front gate. Number seven Oakwood Road. She got out of the car and took in the scene. This was her childhood home, the fine old Victorian family house that she had at times loved, and at times hated for its austerity. Now it looked so different. The bay windows had been removed and replaced with modern black-framed panes of glass, blank and unwelcoming. The trees had been clipped back ruthlessly and the hedge replaced by a red-brick wall. The garden now contained a jumble of outdoor toys, a Wendy-house, climbing frame and swing. A sign above the bright blue front door read in rainbow colours: Oakwood Nursery School. Now, in the late afternoon gloom, there was something unbelievably sad about the abandoned toys in the garden, the lack of lights in the windows. Her parents had sold up several years earlier and moved down to Chesterfield, where Cathy and her husband lived. Erin understood the reasons for the move perfectly; the house was too big for them, and in Chesterfield they could help look after Cathy's youngest, who had autism. And Chesterfield wasn't so very far; less than an hour away by car. But just look at the street now, thought Erin. All those fine old houses - they used to be family homes and were now nearly all converted into flats, offices, nurseries or retirement homes. The heart had gone out of the street, and Erin felt a lump in her throat. She looked up at the first floor windows of her old house - the bedroom where she and Laura had tried on clothes for hours, discarding unsuccessful combinations and throwing them in a heap on the bed. The bathroom where they had tried out ridiculous make-up hints gleaned from teen magazines: pink and plum eye-shadow, blue eye-liner. That feeling of being just on the verge of something exciting, something that would change everything. That was what she missed the most.

She sighed and got back into her car. Excitement! The unexpected! How could she find that again?

But the unexpected can be a double-edged sword. That sudden pump of adrenalin - it can be thrilling, intoxicating - but it can also be terrifying.

Chapter Eleven
The day before the accident

The day started off well enough. Spirits were high as they boarded the train and threw their backpacks onto the luggage racks. Erin and Laura took a seat opposite Karen and Fiona. Karen pulled out a pack of cards and asked what games they all knew.

'Go fish.'

'Old Maid.'

'Snap.'

'Oh, you bunch of wusses, they're all kids' games. Come on, I'll teach you all contract whist. It's easy.'

The three boys had found seats further down the carriage and were teasing each other noisily about something.

'You do!'

'I do not.'

'I know you do.'

'It's you, not me!'

'Shut up! She'll hear you.'

Erin's ears pricked up. She wondered who they were talking about. Laura? Herself? Probably Tara, It's always Tara, she thought.

Tara and Millie were sitting across the aisle, oblivious to the conversation, their heads together, their shoulders hunched and turned towards each other. There was something furtive about their body language, thought Laura, glancing over. She wondered what they were up to. They seemed to be looking down at something in their hands under the table. Tara put something quickly into her jacket pocket, but not quickly enough to prevent Laura seeing a green bottle cap. A pill bottle? Vitamin pills? Or something more illicit? She should really challenge Tara, ask her what was in her pocket, but knew she did not have the strength. Tara would have an excuse, and then Laura would look like a fool in front of everyone. She decided to keep a close eye on Millie instead.

The train journey passed quickly. They got off at Skipton station and did the short walk through town and over the river to the bus station. As they waited for the Malham bus, Laura noticed that Millie could not sit still. Her legs were jiggling. She got up from the bench, sat down again, got up again. Her eyes, always large, now seemed enormous as she gazed around her.

'Sit down, for God's sake, Millie,' said Tom. 'You're driving me nuts!'

Tara pulled Millie back onto the bench and put an arm round her, whispering something into her ear and giving her shoulders a squeeze. They both giggled. Again Laura wondered what they were hiding.

At last the bus came. They bought tickets and negotiated their way onboard with their bulky backpacks. As the bus wound its way slowly towards their destination, Erin gazed out of the window. Urban streets soon gave way to lush green fields, criss-crossed here and there with dry stone walls and dotted with farmhouses. In the distance, the higher fells were greyish-blue in the morning light. It took less that fifteen minutes to reach the village of Gargrave. They struggled off the bus, dumped their packs on the pavement and looked around. The weather was improving by the minute. Patches of blue sky were breaking through the clouds. Erin took a deep breath of fresh, clean air which held the faintest whiff of cow, and felt her spirits rising. The village was so different in feel from the busy, soot-blackened city they had left behind that morning. Attractive stone cottages lined the road. Tea rooms, galleries and pubs enticed customers in with brightly coloured signs and flags. Erin was itching to explore, but Fiona had other ideas:

'Come on then,' she said. 'Packs on and let's get going. It's this way.'

'We've got loads of time,' complained Tom. 'Can't we have a look round first? Have a beer?'

'No, we should get going now. The weather can change in an instant in the Dales,' said Fiona in her rather bossy teacher's voice. 'We need to get the tents up while it's dry. I've got the map. Follow me everyone!'

Tom scowled his displeasure, but reluctantly they fell into step behind Fiona.

They walked along the street towards the Leeds-Liverpool canal, where they leaned over the pretty stone bridge to watch a narrowboat negotiating the lock gates below. They continued along the road for a few hundred metres, then branched off onto the Pennine Way. The path led upwards over grassy meadows of startlingly bright green, crossing several stiles. Simon struggled noticeably as the path grew steeper, and started to lag behind, panting. Karen hung back to join him, and offered to swap backpacks with him, taking his heavier one with the tent strapped underneath. They had a scary moment passing through a field of young cows, which blocked the path and stared at them blankly, immobile and threatening. Erin wasn't sure if they were heifers or bullocks, and wanted to skirt around the edge of the field, but Tom clapped his hands and shouted 'Go on, git!', and one by one they backed away and turned.

'God, you're braver than me!' said Erin, admiringly.

'The trick is not to run,' shrugged Tom. 'Just walk slowly. If you run, they'll run after you. They just want to play.'

'How do you know that?' asked Hamza. 'Are you a cow expert?'

'My uncle's a farmer. Mind you, my aunt once got rolled on by a cow and broke her leg, so you never know.'

Erin held her breath until they were safely into the next field.

After a few hundred metres, the Pennine Way dipped down to meet the road, and a little further on, the signpost guided them through a gate and over a footbridge to reach the banks of the river Aire. They followed the gently flowing water upstream, as it ran between the banks of sycamore, ash and hawthorn. Here the walking was much easier, the only danger being the occasional tree root sticking up from the path, and even Simon managed to keep up a good pace. They walked in single file, enjoying the soothing lapping sound of the river and watching parent ducks shepherd their troops of ducklings through the reeds and under the branches of overhanging trees. The path crossed and recrossed the river over wooden or stone bridges, and then unexpectedly opened out into parkland.

'Let's stop here to eat our sandwiches,' suggested Fiona. 'We're over half way there now.'

They shrugged off their packs and lay their coats on the damp grass. Erin had stuck closely to Laura for most of the morning, aware that her friend still felt raw and uncertain after the gossip incident. But now she noticed Tara sitting alone for a change, and went over to join her. Millie was running up and down the river bank, chasing moorhens.

'Hi.'

'Ah, so you've chosen to talk to me at last, have you?' asked Tara, lifting an eyebrow.

'I wasn't ignoring you. It's just, well, I felt I had to look after Laura a bit. She's still a bit down today.'

Tara shrugged. 'That's not my problem.'

'Besides, Millie's been sticking to you like a limpet all day.'

'Yeah, she's a good kid. But I'd much rather spend time with you.' Tara's green eyes held hers for a long moment, and Erin felt strangely uncomfortable, but at the same time thrilled. Her heartbeat quickened and she knew she was going red. She broke eye contact and quickly delved into her backpack for her packet of ham sandwiches. She peeled back the clingfilm and took a bite. Partly to change the subject, she asked:

'I've been thinking about what you said about paganism the other day. It sounds sort of cool and modern, but it gets such a bad rap in the old films. I want to know more about it. I mean, do you really have those rituals and things? Do you believe in the supernatural? Make sacrifices?'

'Well, it's complicated. There's loads of different types of paganism, just like there's loads of types of Christianity. You could be a Wicca, or a Druid or a Heathen. I guess I'd call myself a Feminist Pagan. I believe in the power of the female. Some pagans get together in groups but most of us do our own thing. So no, I don't do ritual sacrifices and all that crap. But I do mark the seasons, follow the sun, the moon, the tides.'

'And there are gods?'

'Every pagan is a bit different. You find your own thing. That's what's good about it; you don't follow anyone else, you find what works for you. And for me, the divine spirit is in nature. The wind, the leaves, the ocean. The energy that comes from all that.'

'What about the supernatural? Do you believe in the afterlife?'

Tara paused, and looked around her. 'Yes, I think the spirits of the dead are still around us. Most of the time. Even now.' Erin followed Tara's gaze and shivered, imagining the ghostly shapes of her dead grandparents watching her every move. She hadn't been particularly fond of her grandfather; he'd been grumpy and loud and had shouted at her grandmother far too often.

'Can you feel them?'

'Yes, sometimes.'

'And what about powers? Can you see into the future? Can you change things?'

'I sometimes think I can see the future. I have these flashes. I see something, an animal, a cloud, and suddenly it's like I have a feeling. I'm certain something will happen. But it's not all the time. I can't control it. Not yet anyway.'

'What about the future of this weekend? Tonight? Tomorrow?'

A frown creased Tara's brow and she looked unsure for the first time. 'Something is going to happen. But I don't know what.'

'Maybe you'll get off with Tom again!' said Erin, trying to mask her hurt feelings with a smile.

'Nah, not Tom. Maybe someone else...' Tara smiled enigmatically and touched Erin lightly on the arm. 'So are you going to become a pagan, then? Like me?'

'Maybe. Where do I start?'

'I'll pass you my copy of the Idiots Guide to Paganism,' Tara joked. 'No, just think a lot, keep looking at nature, follow your feelings.'

'Right. I will.' Erin was beginning to feel out of her depth in the conversation, so changed the subject again. 'I like your walking boots,' she said. 'Are they new?'

Tara glanced down at her expensive-looking blue and grey Gore-Tex boots. 'Yeah,' she said and angled one foot back and forth so Erin could admire them.

'Where'd you get them? They're really cool.'

'I nicked them.'

'No! Really? God, Tara! How did you get away with that?'

'I've had a lot of practice,' she smirked. 'It's easy, you go shopping with your oldest, naffest shoes on, and a bag that you don't mind leaving behind. Then you say you want to see the colours of the new ones in the daylight – and you just keep walking.'

'God, you've got so much nerve. I'd never dare.'

'Come to Leeds with me next week. I'll nick you some stuff. Shoes are easy; they don't have those ink tags.'

'Oh, um... maybe.' Erin thought longingly of those burgundy Doc Martens. Tempting. 'How much were yours supposed to be?'

But before Tara could answer, Millie flopped down beside them, giving Erin an unfriendly look, and the conversation came to an end.

'I'll go sit with Laura again. She's got Kit Kats,' said Erin, and went to join her friend.

When everyone had finished eating, they set off along the path once again. A few clouds began to appear on the horizon, and a breeze ruffled the grass.

Subtly, the landscape started to change. The trees thinned out and then disappeared. The lush green grass gave way to rougher pasture, studded with clumps of tall moor-grass. As the path climbed steeply uphill, they noticed for the first time the imposing limestone cliff of Malham Cove in the distance. They all stopped to stare. It looked enormous, forbidding, a great slash of pale grey rising up from the valley below.

'We're not going up there tomorrow, are we?' said Erin. 'It looks way too high. It looks dangerous! How do you even get up there?' She felt her skin prickle with trepidation. Danger. Fall. Shit!

'Don't worry,' said Fiona. 'We can all do it. It's not difficult at all. I did it last year. Come on. We've got at least another hour to go to get to the campsite. Let's get going.'

***

It wasn't really a campsite. The Cross Keys Farm was a working sheep farm about a mile outside the little village of Malham. Sheepdogs barked wildly when they pushed open the steel gate and walked up the rutted path to the old farmhouse. Four shabby static caravans stood in a field to the right, their curtains faded and windows rusted. A middle-aged man in blue overalls opened the farmhouse door and looked them up and down briefly. Behind him, they caught a glimpse of an old-fashioned kitchen, dirty plates crowding the square white sink, a rag-rug on the floor.

Fiona stepped forward and began to introduce herself, but the man interrupted.

'Nah then. I see you got here all right. You can put your tents up over there.' He pointed to a patch of land over to the right, near a copse of trees. 'The toilet block is behind the barn. You can build a fire but make sure you put it out before you go to sleep. No noise after eleven o'clock, and when you go, make sure you take all your rubbish with you. You can pay me tomorrow morning.'

With that, he turned his back to them and went back into the farmhouse.

'Well!' exclaimed Fiona. 'He wasn't very friendly. I hope the toilets are ok. It's not at all what I expected...' She looked crestfallen, all her bossy confidence gone.

'Don't worry,' said Karen, putting a comforting arm around Fiona, aware that she was feeling disappointed and personally responsible for the poor welcome. 'We're here, that's all that matters. We don't need posh toilets, it'll be great! Come on, let's see if the boys really know how to put the tents up.'

It took some time and a lot of debate, but eventually the three tents were erected, even if the larger one seemed to sag alarmingly between the tent poles.

'Who's sleeping where?' asked Tom, giving a hopeful glance towards Tara.

'You three boys can take that crappy big tent,' said Fiona. 'I'll go in the orange one with Laura and Erin. Is that OK? And Karen can go with Tara and Millie in the blue one.'

They stuffed their backpacks inside and unrolled their sleeping bags, then split up to search for dry firewood, which they then stacked in a pyramid, ready for the night-time. Hamza produced a tennis ball, and the boys and Karen wandered further down the field to play a noisy game of dodgeball.

Erin and Laura went to check out the toilet block. It was a utilitarian concrete outbuilding, cold and unwelcoming. The windows were dirty and the single electric light cast a yellowish glow onto the facilities. The showers were coin-operated and separated from the central corridor by flimsy shower curtains, their hems black with mould. There appeared to be nowhere to hang a towel or clothes. There were four toilets, but one of them seemed to be leaking, judging by the puddle of water seeping under the door onto the concrete floor. Two bars of soap lay by the single sink; both cracked and streaked with dirt. However, the water from the hot tap was boiling hot.

'Fiona's going to go ape when she sees this!' said Erin. They looked at each other, then both burst into giggles, imagining Fiona's shocked face.

They ate a strange mixture of foods that evening, throwing together everything each had brought and cooking it on the two camping stoves. Spaghetti hoops with cocktail sausages and instant mash potato, with a few baked beans, instant noodles and pasta. Erin found the food strangely delicious. So different from the standard meat and two vegetables her mum cooked at home. After washing up, they lit the campfire and told ghost stories, as the sky darkened all around them and an owl hooted in the trees. After a while, they noticed that Millie was shivering, or more precisely, shaking, and Karen helped put her to bed.

'I hope she's OK,' she said, sitting back down again. 'I think she's coming down with something. She was really hot and sweaty.'

'She's probably just caught a chill. It's pretty cold out here now,' said Tara.

Tom produced a bottle of vodka and Simon some brandy, which they passed round. The atmosphere became warm and relaxed as the alcohol took hold.

'I know,' said Karen, when the ghost stories started to peter out. 'Let's play Truth or Dare. It's what everyone's supposed to do round the campfire.'

'OK,' agreed Tom. 'But what's the penalty if you don't tell the truth?'

'Um… Strip to your undies and run round the campfire?'

'OK, you're on. Who's got the first question?'

'Me,' said Karen. 'One for Fiona. Have you ever peed in a swimming pool?'

Fiona had drunk enough vodka to let her inhibitions down. 'Yes I have!' she declared, and everyone hooted with laughter. It was so unlike prim Fiona. 'When I was much, much younger, I used to do it all the time. My turn now. Simon, who's your celebrity crush?'

'Oh, that's easy. Julia Roberts. Um, Laura. Have you ever... have you ever...' He scratched his head. 'I know, have you ever farted in a lift?'

'No, I haven't, actually. I don't think so. Not in a lift anyway. Lots of other places. OK, one for Tara.' Do I dare, do I dare? thought Laura. Yes, damn it. I'm going to call her out. 'Tara, do you take drugs?'

There was an audible intake of breath. Tara stared coolly at Laura, quite unperturbed by the question. 'Yes, I do.' Another gasp. All heads turned to stare at Tara, but she flicked her hair over her shoulder and stared right back, daring them to comment.

'And did you give drugs to M...?' Laura began to ask, but was cut off mid-sentence.

'Only one question. You've had your go. My turn.' Tara's eyes gleamed in the firelight. 'Hamza, do you fancy Laura?'

Ooh, nasty, thought Erin. Tara had really hit Laura's Achilles heel with that question. She began to consider, for the first time, that Laura might be right about Tara. She could be cruel. Tom was sniggering. All eyes turned to Hamza, as he slowly stood up and unzipped his jacket.

Laura's face burned with embarrassment and her eyes pricked with tears. She felt totally exposed. She itched to run away, to zip herself inside the tent and escape the pitying looks, but forced herself to sit still.

Hamza pulled off his jacket and jumper and started to unbutton his flies. 'But I do think Laura's the nicest person in the group,' he said, giving Laura a shy smile. 'She's lovely.' He yanked off his jeans, hopping unsteadily on one foot, then ran round the campfire amid whoops of encouragement and laughter. 'My question now,' he said, when he was at last sitting back down. He tried to bring the game back from the brink and lighten the mood. 'Tom, have you ever cheated in an exam?'

'Yes, I have. I wrote some equations on my arm for O-level maths last year. I got an A too!'

'Tom! That's shocking! Maybe you're not such a brainbox after all. Your go.'

'Who's left? Karen and Erin? Um... Erin, how many times have you kissed a boy?'

'I've only been kissed the once. And it was a pretty rubbish kiss too!' That'll teach him to snigger at Laura, thought Erin. 'Karen, if we were all in a boat and it was sinking, which of us would you push out first?'

'Ooh, good question... I don't know...'

'It should be me, I'm the heaviest.'

'No, definitely not you, Simon. I know, I'd jump out myself. I'm a really good swimmer. You lot could stay on the boat and sink, and I'd swim to shore.'

It was past eleven o'clock now, the fire was almost dead and the vodka and brandy bottles were empty.

Fiona stood up and said she was going to bed. Karen stood up too, and the two of them fetched torches and made their way to the toilet block. The three boys went to their tent to continue some dice game, leaving Tara, Laura and Erin sitting by the glowing embers of the fire. Tara lit a cigarette and blew out a steady stream of smoke in Laura's direction.

'Are you coming to bed, Erin?' asked Laura.

'Yes, in a minute,' said Erin. 'I'll just sit a bit longer until the fire is completely out.'

Laura made her way alone to the tent, crawled into her sleeping bag and finally let the tears fall. How can Erin still sit with her, still be in thrall to her, after that? she thought. Tara's a nasty, manipulative bitch! She takes drugs! I hate her. I fucking hate her!

Laura shivered inside her sleeping bag. Her feet were freezing. Finding her torch, she reached for her backpack and rooted around, looking for a second pair of socks. Her hand touched something strange. Something scratchy and heavy. What on earth was that? Had her mother sneaked a surprise into her pack? Chocolates maybe? She pulled the object out and shone the torch onto it. It was Fiona's pink sequinned purse, the one that contained the money for the campsite, the one that Fiona would undoubtedly be looking for tomorrow morning.

Laura knew instantly what had happened. How that purse had come to be in her pack. Tara. Another of her sick tricks to isolate her from the others. She must have put it there when they were all collecting firewood. She imagined what would have happened in the morning, with Fiona panicking, everyone searching. She imagined herself explaining to Fiona: 'I didn't take it! Honestly! Someone must have put it there.' She visualised the faces of the group, staring at her, bemused. Would they have believed her?

She quickly put the purse back inside Fiona's pack before she came back from the toilet block and crawled back inside the sleeping bag. Her fists were clenched and her jaw was tight. She shut her eyes and focused all her hatred onto a single person. What if the power of thought could make things happen? What if I could wish something into being? If I concentrate hard enough, maybe...

I wish she would die. I wish she would just fuck off and die!

Die, Tara, just bloody well die!

The tent flap unzipped and Fiona came in. Laura faked sleep.

***

Tara and Erin sat staring into the dying embers.

'You don't really take drugs, do you?' asked Erin at last.

'God, Erin, you're such a baby. Haven't you ever wanted to experiment? Yeah I've taken drugs. Magic mushrooms, LSD...'

'LSD? Bloody hell! But why?'

'It's no big deal. It's cool. Drugs make you experience things that you can't normally see. You can hear the wind talking, whispering things to you. You can see all the different colours in the sky. It makes you aware of every little thing. The grass growing. The wings of bees beating. It brings me closer to nature and makes me feel…. just blown away by the incredible beauty of everything.'

'But it's dangerous! What about bad trips?'

'It's not dangerous if you know what you're doing. If you're in a good place. You want to try?'

'You mean now?'

'Yes. I've got something with me.'

'God! Um… No, I don't think so. I'm not… I'm not ready for that.'

'OK, no pressure.'

They sat for a while longer, and Erin tried to assimilate the new information. This was a long way outside her experience, and she wasn't sure what to think. Did it make Tara more cool, exciting, daring, or did it in fact do the opposite? Make her a loser? Someone at the start of a downward spiral? Was Laura right? Had Tara given drugs to Millie? Surely that couldn't be true.

Suddenly she felt her hand being grasped. Tara's thumb was stroking her palm. She looked up in surprise. Tara's eyes locked onto hers.

'Have you ever kissed a girl?' asked Tara, leaning in a little closer and reaching out her other hand to play with a strand of Erin's hair.

Erin was frozen, transfixed. 'No,' she stuttered.

'Do you want to?'

'I…uh… you're not gay, are you?'

Tara laughed. 'I'm not gay. I'm not straight. I'm not anything. You can't put me in a pigeon-hole. I'm free. I am whatever I want to be, whenever I want to be. And right now I want to kiss you.' The hand that had been playing with Erin's hair crept round the back of her head, and gently pulled Erin towards her. Erin looked into the green eyes, hypnotised, helpless. Tara's eyelids lowered and her mouth was inches away.

'No, don't!' Erin yelped, and pulled away.

Tara's eyes narrowed.

'I'm sorry, I'm just not…'

Tara's expression was suddenly cold. She pushed Erin away. 'I thought you were different. I thought you had some adventure in you,' she spat. 'You're no different from the others. Go back to your boring little friend. Go on. Fuck off to bed, little girl!'

'I'm sorry, I didn't mean to. I mean, I'm flattered, really I am. It's just…'

'Go!'

As Erin stumbled towards her tent and unzipped the flap, she heard Tara's voice:

'Tom? You still awake? Come out here and join me by the fire. I need warming up.'

Chapter Twelve
The day of the accident

Erin woke up to the sound of the wind battering against the side of the tent, making the fabric snap and billow alarmingly. The inside of the tent felt moist. It must have rained in the night. Where her backpack had leant against the canvas wall, a large wet patch had formed on the ground sheet. She pulled one arm from the sleeping bag and tentatively felt around her. There were her jeans. Damp and cold. Damn, her only pair. Her boots, luckily, were upright with her socks tucked inside. She looked at her watch. Eight o'clock. Trying not to wake the others, she inched her way out of the sleeping bag and crawled towards the opening. As she unzipped the tent flap, it flew out of her hands and thrashed into the air, dancing about wildly. A blast of chilly air entered the tent. Erin fought to close the zip again, and eventually succeeded in shutting out the wind. But not before she'd seen the weather outside. Pregnant grey clouds scudded low over the hills, obliterating the tops. The surrounding fields, which yesterday had been a vibrant green in the sunshine, were now monochrome grey. The copse was a waving mass of black limbs. A little part of her was relieved. Surely they would not risk walking on a day like this. They wouldn't go near that ominous cliff face. They could stay around the campsite and relax. She would have the chance to talk to Tara. To make things right again.

She replayed the scene from the previous night. Alone with Tara, in the moonlight, staring into the dying embers and talking. Tara liked her! Really liked her. That was obvious. And she liked Tara. More than that, she needed Tara. Tara had reached out a black-nailed hand and pulled her out of a stagnant, resentful life. She'd lifted her into excitement, danger, the thrill of a grungy kind of glamour. Why had she pulled away? What harm would it have done to experience a kiss? Her second ever kiss? As Tara had leaned towards her, her whole body had responded. She'd felt her heart hammering, her stomach clenching, and every inch of her skin bursting alive with prickles. Was that arousal? Anticipation? Or was it fear? Horror? It was nothing like her reaction to Tom's clumsy kiss. Why hadn't she been brave enough to go through with it? Would there be a second chance? And what would she do if there was? She resolved to speak to Tara a soon as possible.

Gradually the others began to stir, poke their heads out of the tents, stumble off to the toilet block and pull on some clothes. The wind dropped just enough for them to be able to brew tea on the camping stoves and they stood in a circle, shoulders hunched against the cold, drinking the warming liquid. Erin shivered as the wind punched into her wet jeans.

'You look rough,' Simon said to Hamza. 'Is this your first hangover?'

'First time I've ever drunk alcohol. It's haram, it's forbidden. My mum and dad'll kill me. I'm not doing that again. I feel like shit!'

'Don't worry mate, we all feel like shit. You don't have to tell your parents. It's our secret.'

Fiona turned to Millie. 'You look a lot better today, Millie,' she said. 'How do you feel?'

'I'm fine. Why, what's the fuss?'

'You were all shivery last night, you looked really out of it. Like you were coming down with a fever.'

'Well, I'm fine now. It was probably just something I ate.' Her lips curved in a secret smile.

Laura looked over at Tara, gauging her reaction, but she seemed impassive. Tom was standing close behind her, a smug expression on his face.

Erin also glanced over at Tara, trying unsuccessfully to catch her eye. As she looked, Tom slung an arm over her shoulder, in a proprietorial manner. Erin expected Tara to shrug him off with a smart put-down, and was surprised when she didn't. Oh-oh, she thought. So that's how it is. She's back with Tom. A wave of misery engulfed her.

'What are we going to do today?' asked Karen. 'The weather's shit. It must have been raining loads in the night – look at all the puddles. And those clouds look pretty menacing. I'm sure it's going to bucket down again.'

'Let's stay here,' said Tom. 'I can think of a few things to do.' He winked at Tara, suggestively.

'No way,' said Fiona. 'We didn't come all this way just to hang out inside the tents. Where's your spirit of adventure? We'll walk to Janet's Foss, and Goredale Scar. That's an easy walk. And if the weather looks a bit better when we get there, we'll go on to Malham Cove.'

'Won't it be a bit dangerous with all the rain and the wind?'

'Look, it's such a well-known walk. There'll be loads of other people doing it. I've done it before with my parents. The car park's always rammed. You even see little kids doing it. Women in flip-flops. It's a doddle. Come on, let's organise some breakfast. Who's got the bread? And the jam? Laura and Erin, you make the sarnies. I'm off to pay the farmer.'

Fiona climbed back inside her tent to fetch the money, and Laura watched Tara intently. Tara had lost her habitual indifferent expression. Her eyes followed Fiona with an amused gleam. When Fiona emerged with the pink purse, Tara's gaze shot to Laura, her eyes narrowed. Laura crossed her arms and replied with a sardonic smile, all her suspicions confirmed. Tara shrugged and turned away.

One hour later they set off with Fiona in the lead, brandishing the map, chin held high and striding ahead with confidence. It always surprised Erin to see Fiona walk or run. Her legs were short and chunky, and she seemed to take twice as many steps as Karen or Laura did, but she covered the ground with speed. The others followed with more reluctance, bundled into anoraks, woolly hats and scarves. Erin trudged down the rutted path next to Laura, trying to avoid the rain-filled potholes. Neither of them talked.

They picked up the Pennine Way again and set off along the east side of the river, which was now engorged and frothy with the overnight rain. Leaving the path, they walked through a gate and into dark, ancient woodland. They found themselves in a kind of secret, emerald-green dell. The contrast was sudden and enchanting. The path wound through tall, moss-covered trees that dripped onto their hats as the sudden gusts shook the leaves. The air was thick with the pungent scent of wild garlic.

'Hey, stop, look!' called Tara suddenly, pointing to something poking out of the lush grass.

Fiona turned back. 'What is it?'

'A money tree!'

They all crowded round and examined the huge log at the side of the path. Hundreds of coins had been hammered into the bark. Some looked very old, greenish and twisted, others were shiny and new. Tom knelt down and tried to tug a few coins out, but Tara slapped his arm away.

'What is that?'

'It's pagan,' explained Tara. 'People make an offering to the forest or the spirits that live here. If you put a coin in the tree you get safe passage. Who's got a coin? We can knock it in with a rock.'

Millie jumped up and down excitedly. 'Yes, let's,' she said.

'We'll do nothing of the sort! What a load of rubbish,' Fiona snapped.

'Do you really want to defy the spirits?'

'Oh, shut up, Tara! All this pagan talk is driving me nuts. Superstitious nonsense. Sacrificing a coin to the spirits? You can't seriously believe that.'

'But actually, I think we should...' Tara looked strangely nervous.

'No!' For once, Fiona stood her ground and squared up to Tara, her jaw set. Behind her thick-lensed glasses her pale eyes were determined. 'It's childish bollocks. Anyway, we're wasting time. Let's get going.'

'But what harm can it do?' began Tara, but Fiona had already turned away and was striding towards the waterfall. Simon shrugged his shoulders and followed. Then, Hamza and Karen, and lastly Tom.

'Stupid fucking cow,' hissed Tara. She took something out of her pocket and held it tightly in her fist, her lips moving silently as she stared after Fiona. Then she released her fingers. Something small and dust-like fell to the ground, like crushed leaves or herbs.

Laura and Erin, standing just behind, exchanged worried glances. 'Shit!' breathed Laura. 'What was all that about? Did she just cast a spell or something? I don't like this. Not on top of the Ouija board. I've got the creeps.'

'Fuck knows. But this whole day seems weird to me. We're all hungover, the weather's awful, Fiona's being bossy and no-one's really enjoying themselves. I've got a bad feeling.'

'Me too. Well, let's stay close. We'll be OK if we stick together.'

The sound of rushing water grew louder and louder as they rounded the last few bends. And then there it was, Janet's Foss. They stared. The noise was deafening. The waterfall was not very high, but the amount of water thundering over the rocks and hurling itself into the pool at its foot was spectacular. A few other groups of walkers had gathered here, some taking photos, some even removing their shoes to dip their feet in the pool. Fiona pointed and shouted something, but her words were lost in the roar. They watched the water forming patterns of white and peaty brown as it smashed against the mossy rocks in the plunge pool and tumbled further down the river. After a few minutes, Fiona beckoned them to continue and they set off up a steep path to the left of the falls. They walked past a campsite, which looked a lot more inviting than the one they had left that morning.

'Hey, Fiona,' called Simon. 'Why aren't we staying here? It looks great!'

'Too expensive,' replied Fiona. 'And probably booked solid anyway. Come on. Goredale Scar's this way.'

They followed a broad gravelled path which snaked along beside the river through a desolate-looking valley, strewn with boulders and moss. To the left and right, high cliffs rose hundreds of feet into the air, with stunted blackened trees clinging tenaciously to the sides. Here and there, tumbles of scree scarred the cliffs. The walking was easy, but they were more exposed to the wind here, which battered at their anoraks and made them billow. And then the rain started, coming across the valley in slanting waves, drenching their legs and dripping off their hoods. On and on they trudged, heads down. They crossed a few other groups of bedraggled walkers coming in the opposite direction, and exchanged rueful smiles. The gorge, at first open, became gradually steeper, higher and narrower as they progressed. The colours changed too; at first the valley floor was green, with clumps of grass, moss and the occasional twisted tree, but the further they went, the more all colour disappeared, leaving only the grey and black of the rocks all around. The gorge became steadily more enclosed, until eventually they were walking in the dark shadow of the overhanging cliffs, towering over three hundred feet above them. It felt other-worldly, claustrophobic, like a film set from a Sci-Fi movie. Rounding the last corner, they came to the waterfall, rearing up in a spectacular double cascade, blocking their way. It was much bigger than the previous one, gushing over huge boulders in every direction with magnificent force.

Protected from the elements by the overhang, they stopped and ate biscuits with numb fingers. After a few minutes the rain began to ease, then finally stopped. The group split up and began to wander off in different directions to explore this alien landscape. Hamza and Karen decided to climb partway up the waterfall.

'Watch out, it'll be really slippery!' warned Fiona.

'We'll be careful,' they called.

Erin and Laura had wandered up the valley a little way, admiring the way the water had carved smooth, curved hollows into the rocks. They chatted easily, but then, looking back, Erin saw that Tara was sitting alone on a rock and lighting a cigarette. Sensing that this was her moment to talk, she turned and picked her way back down between the boulders to join her, leaving Laura staring after her.

But Tom got there first. He flopped down close beside Tara and threw an arm round her shoulders.

'Give us a kiss?' he said.

Erin stopped in her tracks, embarrassed and unsure whether to continue.

'Fuck off, Tom,' said Tara, lazily, blowing a string of smoke rings into the air.

'What?' Tom's mouth hung open in astonishment. 'But we…'

'Just because we had sex in the toilet block doesn't mean I like you,' said Tara, coolly. 'You can go away now.'

'You…you…' stammered Tom.

'You should thank me, really. You're not a virgin any more. But don't read anything into it. I wanted sex and you were there. Go on, fuck off now.'

Tom stood up and stumbled away, and as he brushed past Erin, he glanced up at her. She could see that his face was aflame with humiliation and anger. 'Fucking bitch! Fucking bitch!' she heard him mutter to himself. She felt sorry for him, but also felt a little spark of hope. Tara didn't want him. She'd just used him. Maybe it's still me she wants. Maybe there was still a chance to make things right with her. She made her way carefully down the last few metres to where Tara was sitting.

'Can we talk?' she asked.

Instead of replying, Tara sighed and stood up. She slowly and deliberately crushed out her cigarette with the toe of her walking boot. Her eyes never left Erin's as she mashed the cigarette into the ground. Then she walked right up to her, and pushed straight past her, making Erin stumble backwards. She had been dismissed.

Laura stood above, watching the scene play out. Erin, you idiot, she thought. Why do you keep going back to her? What is this awful magnetism that Tara has? Again, fiercely, she repeated her mantra: 'I wish she was dead, I wish she was dead.'

'Come back down now,' Fiona called up to Karen and Hamza, halfway up the waterfall. 'We need to decide what to do next.'

'What are the options?' asked Simon, when the group had reassembled. 'Back to the campsite?' he added hopefully. 'Pub?'

'No, the weather's not bad now. The rain's stopped. We're going to Malham Cove.'

'Really? But the weather could change again. I think we should go back,' said Laura, remembering the 'Danger, Fall' warning. She glanced uneasily at the sky. It did seem to be clearing up.

'No, we're nearly there, it'd be a shame to miss it. It's easy, I promise. But there's two ways to go. One way is to climb up the waterfall and on to Malham Tarn, and then down to the Cove. The other way is to go back the way we came for a bit, and then there's a path off to the right. If the weather stays like this, I think we'll be fine. What does everyone think?'

'No way I'm climbing up that waterfall,' said Simon. 'It looks too hard for me.'

'Yes, it's not very easy,' Karen confirmed. 'It's dead slippery. We should take the other path.'

'OK. Let's go then.'

They retraced their steps back through the gorge, and as it

opened out once more, became aware of a thin sun casting a pale glow behind the purple clouds. Passing an arched stone bridge, they found the footpath leading to the Cove. It was a steep track leading up through open countryside. The wet grass soaked into their boots as they followed a dry stone wall uphill. Simon stopped frequently, puffing out his cheeks and wiping the sweat from his forehead. Millie was lagging behind too, and Karen and Hamza each took one of her hands to pull her up the incline. The grass grew rougher and wirier as they climbed. They saw the first outcrops of limestone on the hilltops, standing like sentinels, guarding the path. Sheep stared at them, outlined against the darkening sky. At the top of the hill they passed, one by one, through a wooden gate and there it was: the limestone pavement.

It was extraordinary, too vast to take in. If the gorge had felt like a film set, this felt like something from a different planet, a moonscape maybe, barren and bleak. The huge expanse of rock had been carved into an army of uneven, jutting lumps, with deep, black crevices separating each. Delicate flowers eked out a meagre existence between the inhospitable slabs. One solitary twisted ash tree provided the only visual relief in this grey-washed, exposed arena.

They picked their way slowly over the pavement, choosing each step with care. The rocks were slick and shiny with rain. Some were loose and wobbled as they stepped on them. Puddles lay in the hollows. They were aware that one slip could result in a broken ankle, or worse. There were only a handful of other people on the pavement. Some had ventured right to the very edge of the precipice to admire the view of the valley below. Others were making their way to the far side, where the steps led down to the base of the cliff.

Laura glanced nervously at the sky. The sun had disappeared and layer upon layer of purplish-grey clouds were massing overhead, the topmost clouds almost black. In the distance she saw diagonal streaks of rain, falling a few miles away, curving in the wind. She shivered. One by one, the other groups of walkers looked up, frowned and began to drift off until they were quite alone on the pavement.

'Hey! You've got to see this view,' Karen called to them. She had made it to the very edge. 'Don't stay so far back, you're missing the best bit.'

'It's dangerous. There's no barrier, nothing to stop you falling,' yelled Fiona.

'Come on, if you go slowly it'll be fine. It's incredible!'

Tom, Hamza and Tara carefully negotiated the jigsaw of rocks until they, too, were standing at the edge. They sat, dangling their legs over the precipice. Erin noticed that Tom chose to sit as far away from Tara as possible.

'Wow, oh wow! What a view! Come on, the rest of you, it's OK. Someone hang on to Millie, though.'

Erin and Laura glanced at each other nervously. Danger, fall – the words rang in Laura's ears.

'I don't think we should...' she began.

Erin shrugged. 'We've come all this way. We might as well see the view.'

'You go. I'm not going anywhere near it.'

'I'm staying here with Millie,' called Simon. 'I don't trust her not to throw herself over.'

Erin took a few steps closer, staring at her feet, aware that her legs were trembling. This was a test of courage, a kind of initiation rite. She wanted desperately to be included in the brave group.

'You can do it!' called Tom. 'Nearly there.'

Laura and Fiona stayed back, Fiona shaking her head and tutting in disapproval.

Step by cautious step. Then there were no more rocks. Just a void. A perfect vertical drop of several hundred feet to the valley below. It would be so easy to fall, tempting almost, just one more step... Erin felt the sickly churn of vertigo take hold of her body. She swayed slightly.

'Sit down, quick,' said Tom, and reached out a hand to help her.

Sitting beside her four friends, the vertigo started to recede and Erin could at last open her eyes. Crows cruised at eye-level and below them, riding the breeze and cawing to each other. A bigger bird, was it a falcon, wheeled overhead. They could see for miles: the snake of the beck, the white gravel path which followed it, the lush green valley dotted with rocks, the clumps of trees and the dry stone walls criss-crossing the low hills. In the very distance the fells were blue, and the sky was clear. It was a scene of tranquillity, a kind of unspoilt Eden. They sat for almost half an hour, silent, admiring, unaware that behind them, the clouds were rolling in at alarming speed.

Fiona broke the spell. 'Come back now,' she called. 'We're going to be in the clouds soon. We should get going.'

Still they lingered, unable to look away. Fiona reluctantly picked her way over to them. 'Look behind you!' she said. 'We won't be able to see a thing if we stay longer.'

As she spoke, fingers of hill fog reached towards them, damp and insidious.

'Come on!' said Fiona again, nervous now. 'The steps down are over there to the right. We need to go.'

The mist was suddenly thick, surrounding them completely, then rolling off the edge of the cliff. The air was heavy with suspended raindrops which clung to their hair and clothes.

Pulling their hoods over their heads, they began to stand and inch away from the edge. Erin could just about make out the outline of Simon, standing a few metres away. She could no longer see Laura. Then she could no longer see anyone at all.

***

The stone steps down were a nightmare. Four hundred of them, steep and slippery, hard to make out in the mist. It was impossible to see the valley below, which was probably a blessing; it forced them to concentrate only on the next footstep, then the one after, placing each with acute focus. With their hoods pulled tight against the damp, they looked neither up, nor round, but plodded on with desperate determination. Millie was scared and Karen was guiding her down extremely cautiously, pointing to each step and holding out a hand. Simon's knees were aching and he was sweating profusely. He took each step slowly, placing his right foot down, then swinging his left foot to join it on the same step before attempting the next one. Inevitably, the group became strung out.

When she at last reached the bottom, Erin looked round for Laura. There she was, behind Simon, patiently taking the last few steps.

'God, that was awful!' said Laura, when she reached her. 'My legs are shaking. Where are the others?'

They looked around. And saw no-one. 'They must have gone on ahead.'

'They could have waited,' said Simon, joining them. 'Miserable buggers!'

'Yeah. But it's obvious where the path goes. We'll soon catch them up.'

Before starting, the three of them paused for a long moment to stare up at the semi-circle of rock towering above them. All they could see was a grey-streaked vertical wall, dotted with stunted trees, disappearing into a sea of cloud which seeped over the top and around the edges. From the base, the beck flowed happily from a narrow slit of cave, the only sign of life.

It was about a mile along a flat, gravelled path which followed the river. Simon, Laura and Erin walked abreast, taking their time. When they came to the gate leading to the road, they saw the others at last.

'Thanks for waiting!' complained Simon, placing one hand on the gate and panting.

'Sorry, you lot were too slow,' said Tom with a smirk.

'Well, at least we all made it. That was quite an adventure!'

said Karen.

'It was a killer! My legs are still aching.'

'We deserve a drink. Is there a pub in Malham?'

'Yeah, there's two or three, I think. Good idea.'

'Wait a minute.' This was Simon, suddenly serious. 'There's someone missing.'

'Shit, yeah.'

'Where's…?'

'Who saw her last?'

'D'you think she's still coming down?'

'Should we go back and look?'

'Was she following you?'

'I didn't see her. Did anyone else?'

'Shouldn't we wait a bit?'

They all talked at once. It was Simon who took charge. Pulling himself upright again, he said: 'We'll split up. Millie's tired, me too. We'll wait here in case she comes from another direction. Tom, Karen, Hamza, you're the fittest. Run back to the cliff and look.'

'Should we go back up the steps?'

'No, I don't think so. It's still dangerous. Go and shout, ask around if there's anyone else still there. Somebody must have seen her.'

Erin chewed the skin around her fingernail nervously as they waited by the gate, scanning the path. It seemed to be taking forever. Rain had started to fall. Figures approached and she straightened up – but no, it was a family, bundled up and dejected, the children dragging their feet and whining.

'We've lost our friend,' said Simon, as they got to the gate. 'Have you seen a girl in a blue jacket?'

'Sorry mate,' the father replied. 'We haven't seen anyone. I think we're the last people there. I hope you find her.'

Then they saw figures approaching again. Just three of them, jogging back along the path.

'No luck?'

'Nothing. What do we do now?'

'We walk to the village, find a phone and contact mountain rescue.' Simon's voice was grim.

'Oh shit, oh shit!'

Erin was shaking. Millie crying.

And Laura had gone pale. 'Oh God,' she thought. 'I didn't mean it! I didn't want to... I never thought...'

PART TWO

Chapter Thirteen

Erin sat on the edge of the desk and surveyed the students. Sixteen fresh faces stared back at her expectantly.

'Right then,' she began. 'Listen up everybody! Last year our focus was on outgoing tourism: the role of the travel agent, the tour operator, the site reps, the hotel, the resort manager, et cetera. This year we're focussing more on inbound tourism. We'll be looking at how to attract tourists to our region. To Yorkshire. Who would come? What are the main attractions? How do we market them? How can we persuade guests to extend their stay?

'A big part of this term is going to be project work and we're going to be making a start on that today. I want you to work in groups of four. Each group will focus on a different aspect of tourism in Yorkshire. You might want to think about the regeneration of our seaside towns. Maybe how to make the most of our industrial heritage. How to exploit the Tour de Yorkshire cycle race, or the Yorkshire Sculpture Park, for example. How to promote sustainable tourism. Your project must consist of a description of the attraction, an analysis of its strengths and weaknesses, and an action plan for a future marketing campaign.

'I also want to use this as an opportunity to develop some real-life, hands-on tourism skills. So in a couple of weeks' time,

I'm going to be asking each group to organise a day trip to your chosen location. You'll be given a set budget and I want you to organise the coach travel yourselves – that means ringing up different companies, getting quotes, et cetera. You will be acting as tour guides on the coach, giving information and answering questions, so make sure you get a coach with a microphone. You'll also be leading the group through the attraction. Right. Any questions?'

The class looked dazed, rather overwhelmed by all the information they had just been given.

'Don't look so worried, I'll give you lots of help. You've got lots of time to prepare. Right then. Today we're going to go down to the computer lab for research. You've got two hours to choose your attraction. At the end of that time I want you to give me a brief outline of what you've chosen and why. OK? Now, organise yourselves in groups of four, please.'

Groups finally decided, Erin shepherded the class out of the classroom and locked the door, then followed them down two flights of stairs to the computer room.

Yes, she thought. I've got a nice easy start to the term. All I have to do is walk up and down, giving a little nudge here and there, getting them on the right track. Sitting down again, she let her thoughts wander.

It had been a strange morning. Walking to her car, she'd remembered that she hadn't checked the post the previous day; the letter box was a joint one for all six houses, situated at the end of the lane, and she often forgot. She'd stopped the car, unlocked her letterbox and retrieved two bills. A piece of blue paper had fluttered to the ground. She picked it up, supposing it was a flyer for something or other. She'd turned it over. Written in large black capitals was the message:

I KNOW WHAT YOU DID!

What the hell's this, she'd thought, crumpling the note and throwing it into the door pocket, where it nested amongst the parking slips and sweet wrappers. Was one of the neighbours upset about her putting the bins out on the wrong day? About Ted taking a sneaky cutting from next-door's lilac tree? She'd put it out of her mind as she drove off towards college, but now her thoughts returned to it. It was a bit creepy. Something about the spikey capitals, the way the pressure of the pen had almost torn a hole through the paper, and the use of an exclamation mark. It seemed somehow... malicious, angry. She decided to show it to Ted when she got home.

An hour and a half later, Erin stood up and clapped her hands, getting everyone's attention.

'OK, everyone, time's getting short. I know I've been round most of you. Have you all decided on something?'

'Yes.' A chorus of nodding heads.

'Ok. Um... Right then. Harry's group, can you tell us about your project, please?'

'We were thinking about the National Coal Mining Museum in Wakefield. It's really brilliant, you get taken down the pit by ex-miners, and get the whole experience underground, but we don't think it's well known outside the area. And it should be. It should be famous, like the slate mines in Wales, for instance.'

'OK, good. That sounds like a really interesting one. Wendy, what have you got?'

'We're thinking about sculpture. There's the Hepworth Gallery in Wakefield and the Yorkshire Sculpture Park in Bretton, which is the biggest and best in Britain. People come for the day, but we think we could develop sculpture weekends, with a three-night hotel stay, for example.'

'Fantastic! And you don't think that's already been done?' Erin was pretty sure it had been, but kept that to herself. There was still plenty of mileage in the project.

'Um.. not sure. But not that we've heard of.'

'OK, good. Susan, what's your team come up with?'

'We want to look at seaside towns like Filey and Whitby. They used to be so popular with families, but a lot of the B&Bs are struggling now. Everyone goes to Spain instead. So we want to find out how to rebrand seaside towns and get the tourists back.'

'Perfect. Good idea. OK, finally, Salim, what's your idea?'

'We want to do Malham Cove.'

'Malham?' Erin's voice came out as a high-pitched squeak and she fought to control it. 'But that's one of the most well-known places in Yorkshire! Does it need any more help attracting tourists? Especially after the Harry Potter film?'

'That's the thing. We want to look at how to stop all the tourists ruining it. How to stop it becoming like a theme park with a massive car park and a million people dropping litter everywhere. So it'd be about sustainable tourism and how you make people responsible.'

Erin's heart sank. Oh shit. The project was good, there was no way she could quash it. She tapped her pen against her teeth, thinking of possible objections. None came. She swore she'd never set foot there again, but this seemed unavoidable.

'OK,' she said finally. 'That will be great. You've all come up with excellent ideas. Right, homework diaries out, please. For next time, I want you to prepare a description of your attraction; the geography, the access routes, population, etc. Some statistics about current visitor numbers, that kind of thing. Have you got all that? Any questions? Right, log out now, switch off, and we'll go back to the classroom for your bags and coats.'

When the students had dispersed with their belongings, Erin sat at her desk again, her chin in her hands. Malham. She dreaded seeing the place again. There would be a coach trip with her students, and she would have to appear calm and in control. Maybe they'd just go to the village and not to the Cove. Could she suggest that? It seemed unlikely. Most of her students had seen the Harry Potter film; they had been talking about it as they climbed the stairs. They would no doubt want to go to the top, to recreate the famous scene and take selfies for their Instagram posts.

Wearily, she collected her files and marker pens, stuffed them in her bag and cleaned the whiteboard. She locked the door and went down to the staffroom for a much needed coffee. She checked her pigeon-hole to see if her photocopies had been placed there by the secretary. Nothing. Only a thin strip of blue paper. Oh God! The same blue paper as earlier that day, this time folded in half. Her heart started hammering again. What the hell? She took it out. This was not a disgruntled neighbour. This was something personal. Someone had been to her house, someone had been to her work. Maybe someone was following her!

She could already see the indentations where tall letters had scoured the paper. She unfolded it and read. She gasped. A hand went up to her throat and she took a step back, nearly colliding with a colleague.

YOU MUST PAY

Her instinct was to crush the paper and throw it in the bin. To get it away from her as quickly as possible. Then she thought: this might be serious. I might need to show this to the police. Gingerly, she placed the note in the side pocket of her bag. Then, forgetting all thoughts of coffee, she ran down the stairs to the entrance, flung open the heavy glass door, fumbled for her car keys in her coat pocket and half-walked-half-ran to where she'd left the car that morning.

Then she stopped and stared. There was something tucked under the windscreen wiper. It wasn't a parking ticket. It was blue. Erin was now shaking, panicking. She hardly dared approach. Her breathing was odd, she felt she couldn't get enough air into her lungs. She leant against the brick wall and waited, forcing her heart to slow and her breathing to return to normal. At last she dared pluck the paper from the windscreen and open it up.

I CAN SEE YOU!

Erin unlocked the car and drove home far too quickly. She ran into the house and locked the door behind her.

She wished, more fervently than ever before, that Ted was there.

KATE LEONARD

She needed her husband.

Chapter Fourteen

'Thanks, Ted, thanks so much for doing that. It's done me so much good.'

'Hey, you don't need to thank me. I enjoyed it too. We should do that kind of thing more often.'

'I'd love to!'

'Are you feeling better now?'

'Yes, much. But I kind of don't want to get home. I don't know what I'll find there. I'm still a bit nervous.'

Ted took one hand off the steering wheel and placed it over Erin's, giving it a squeeze.

'Whatever it is, we'll sort it out. It's probably some sick joke. A student you gave a crap mark to, looking for revenge, that's my guess. They'd have access to your car and your pigeon-hole.'

'But the house?'

'Yellow pages. Easy to find with our surname, there aren't many Dankworths in the phone book.'

'Yeah, I guess. Yes, I'm sure you're right.'

'What was your best bit of the weekend?'

'I enjoyed all of it. Um… just being in the sea air, I think. I feel like it's blown all the crap away. You?'

'Saturday night, definitely.' Ted grinned. He replaced his hand on the steering wheel and hummed happily as they drove through the fading light.

It had been an invigorating weekend. The Airbnb that Ted had booked turned out to be a fisherman's cottage in the little village of Craster, on the Northumberland coast. They'd arrived in the dusk, but already Erin could smell the tang of the sea, as they pulled their holdalls and provisions from the boot of the car. Opening the gate and crossing the paved front garden, they located the key in the safe box and pushed open the door. The interior was a surprise; if the outside was stone-built and traditional, the interior was bright and modern with an open-plan kitchen-living space. They dumped their case in one of the upstairs bedrooms, and unpacked the food.

'Shall I put the lasagne in the oven?' asked Erin.

'No, tell you what, it's only eight o'clock. Bung it in the fridge and let's go to that pub we passed and see if they're still serving food.'

'OK!'

Half and hour later they were sitting in the Lobster Pot, with a crab salad and a steak pie plus two pints of bitter on the table in front of them. Erin breathed a huge sigh.

'This is bliss.'

'Cheers.' Ted touched his glass to hers and took a long pull from his pint.

'Ted, I'm sorry I've been such a bitch lately,' said Erin, picking up her fork. 'I haven't been feeling very happy and I've been taking it out on you. And none of it's your fault, really.'

'Shh. Forget about it. You don't have to explain. Let's just have a fun weekend. What do you want to do? Hadrian's Wall, castles?'

'I want the sea, the sea and more sea! Let's find some nice long walks along beaches.'

And that's what they did. The next morning they woke up to blue skies, although the wind was fierce. They pulled on warm clothes, made up a picnic, and walked along the grassy footpath that wound northwards through farmland, with the rugged coastline to their right. The sea was a vivid blue and agitated. Eider ducks and oystercatchers rootled about by the shoreline, and in the distance they caught what might have been the bobbing heads of seals. The ruined towers of Dunstanburgh Castle appeared over the next rise, standing proudly on a hill, overlooking a huge stretch of sandy beach. Instead of paying the entrance fee, they scrambled down to the beach, gazing into the rockpools, searching for tiny crabs hiding amongst the seaweed. They ate their picnic sitting with their backs to the low cliffs, then strolled along the wide, empty beach, watching the occasional dog owner throw a ball, or tempt their pet into the sea. They stopped for a pint of beer in the village of Low Newton, then retraced their steps back to the cottage. Erin caught sight of her face in the hall mirror as she took off her coat; her skin was glowing and her hair was a tangled mess. She laughed and realised, with a shock, that she was happy.

That evening they ate fish and chips on the harbour wall, watching a full moon rise over the sea, painting the crests of the waves silver. They walked hand in hand back to the cottage, and Ted leant down to kiss her. She tasted vinegar and salt on his lips. She felt an unaccustomed stirring, and put a hand around his neck to prolong the kiss. They shrugged out of their coats clumsily and climbed the stairs. That night they made love, and for the first time in a long while, Erin felt totally engaged. I remember this, she thought. This is real living. Oh God, why can't it be like this every time?

The following day, the weather was bright and cold once more. They checked the tide times on the internet, then drove over the causeway to Holy Island. They walked along windswept beaches, through undulating sand dunes, and over rocky clifftop paths, before exploring Lindisfarne castle and the ghostly ruined priory. They were late coming back over the causeway. The road, which, just that morning had cut through sandy flats intersected by low channels of seawater, was now surrounded by the encroaching waves. Erin gripped the door handle with white knuckles as the car splashed through seawater in the dips, sending up sprays of white. At last they made it to the mainland and she let out her breath.

'Phew! That was a bit touch and go.'

'We must be almost the last ones off,' Ted grinned. 'There's only two cars behind us.'

'Get you, being all adventurous! Not like you to take a risk! That was another great day. I wish we were staying longer.' Erin's mood suddenly plummeted as she realised they would have to pack up and leave soon.

'We'll come back. It's not so far to drive. I was thinking, looking at those people on the beach yesterday... Should we get a puppy d'you think? It'd make us do more walks. Make me, in any case. You walk a lot, but it'd give me a reason to get off my backside a bit more often.'

'Yes! Let's. I like that idea.' Erin was delighted to have a project; she could research the different dog breeds and find a healthy, good tempered, house-friendly, non-chewy puppy to look after. A little creature to add a new dimension to life at home.

This thought kept Erin occupied on the drive back to Wakefield, running through all the pros and cons of owning a dog, but as the car exited the motorway and headed towards the city, her mood darkened. Her thoughts returned to the notes once again.

'Ted, can you stop at the letterbox?' she asked when the car pulled into their lane. 'Can you check the mail for me? I don't want to look.'

'Sure.' Ted got out, leaving the door open, and searched for the little key on his keyring. He opened the letterbox, peered in and turned to give Erin the thumbs up. 'Nothing!' he said. 'Not even a bill.'

'Oof, that's a relief.'

They parked in the driveway and pulled the cases out. The motion-triggered exterior light came on as they got to the front door. Erin gasped and took a step back. Scrawled across the white door in large red letters was a single word.

MURDERER

'Shit,' said Ted, putting the bags on the ground and touching the letters to see if the paint was dry. 'This is not a joke any more. Someone's got it in for you. Should we call the police?'

'Yes. Yes, I think we have to.' Erin was shaking.

'Come on. Let's get you inside.' He put an arm round his wife and guided her through the door, then went back for the bags and locked the door carefully behind him. 'I'll pour us both a whisky, then we'll decide what to do. Have you got classes tomorrow? I could go to the police station with you in the morning.'

'No, I don't start till ten o'clock. We could go before. Should we clean it off?'

'We'll take a photo in the morning. But maybe we should see what the police say. They might want to see it before we clean it.' He pressed a glass into her hand. 'Besides, I'd need to research how you get the paint off. It looked like emulsion, not gloss. Should be OK.'

'I don't want the neighbours to see it. Can't we do something?'

'OK. I'll get some cardboard and tape it over the door first thing. Now, drink your whisky and try to put it out of your mind. It's just a malicious prank. Nothing to worry about.'

Erin looked at her husband. She realised that he had qualities that she relied on; his calm acceptance, his practical nature, his unquestioning faith in her. His solidity in the face of the unexpected. He maybe wasn't the most exciting of men; his predictability often infuriated her, but at that moment he was just what she needed.

'Come on, let's go to bed,' said Ted. 'Don't worry about it any more. I'm here and whatever this is about, we'll sort it.'

As Erin climbed the stairs, she was surprised to see Ted resetting the alarm; something they never usually did while inside the house. He is worried too, she thought, he just doesn't want to show it.

It took her a long time to go to sleep. Each time she shut her eyes, she saw patterns of red against white superimposed on her eyelids. *Murderer*. Why would anyone think that? Who could possibly think that? Did it relate to the accident in Malham?

Laura had warned: 'Don't stir things up.'

What had she done?

Chapter Fifteen

'What should we put for number nine? Heart?'

'No, I'm sure it's skin.'

'What was the question again?'

'What's the largest organ in the human body.'

'OK, you're the nurse, I'll bow to your superior knowledge. Put skin. Are there any other gaps? What was question fifteen?'

'It was something about how many golf courses there are in Scotland. Richard thought two hundred, but Ted thinks it's a lot more. He guessed more like six hundred.'

'Ted's usually right about sport stuff. Put six hundred. Quick, they're coming to collect the papers.'

Laura held the sheet up and the quizmaster added it to his pile. It was half-time in the Friday night pub quiz at the Star Inn. Laura had phoned Ted and suggested they make up a team, and Ted had leapt at the idea, hoping it would distract Erin from her anxiety. There had been no more notes since they got back from Northumberland two weeks ago, but he had noticed a difference in Erin. She was reluctant to answer the phone when it rang. She pulled the blinds down early, well before it was dark. She had asked him to swap cars for a while. She seemed subdued, withdrawn.

There was a half-hour break before the music round. Ted and Richard were at the bar, chatting as they queued for drinks, but the queue was enormous and they would be lucky to get served before the quiz restarted. Erin took the opportunity to fill Laura in on recent events.

'Laura, some shit's been happening and I'm really worried.'

'What? Oh no! Between you and Ted? You seem to be getting on better lately.'

'No. Not Ted. It's…' Erin didn't know where to begin. Instead she pulled out her mobile phone, pressed the gallery icon and showed Laura the first photo of a crumpled piece of blue paper.

'*I know what you did,*' Laura read. 'What does that mean? Where did you get this?'

'It was in my letterbox. Then this one was in my pigeon-hole at college.' She swiped the screen to show Laura the second note.

'*You must pay*. What the fuck?'

'And this was on the windscreen of the car.' She swiped to the next shot. 'And this is the worst of all. This was painted on the front door when we got back from that weekend away.'

'*Murderer*. Bloody hell! Shit, Erin! Have you any idea who…?'

'No!'

'Did you go to the police?'

'Yes, we did. First thing on the Monday after. They took a statement and kept the notes. They came to look at the door. But they said it's just vandalism. I don't even think they fingerprinted the notes. They didn't seem to take it very seriously – you know, they asked the usual questions: had I made any enemies, had I seen anyone hanging around… They just said to let them know if anything else happens.'

'But nothing since then?'

'No, nothing.' She took a deep breath. 'Laura, do you think it could relate to Malham? To the accident?'

'I was wondering the same thing, to be honest. It does seem a coincidence that this happened just after you got back in contact with Simon. But why would anyone think you had anything to do with it?'

'I don't know, I've no idea! It's so fucked-up!'

'Did you get in contact with anyone else from the old group?'

'I put out some friend requests, but Simon's the only one who answered. It can't be him; he lives too far away, in London. He's got a busy life there.'

'You never know… But the friend requests might have triggered the others to look for you, maybe? But why? Why you?'

Laura was perplexed. If anyone should be blamed for the death, it was surely her. She swallowed down the guilt which threatened to rise up again.

'What can I do to help? Do you want me to see if I can get in touch with Karen again? Ask her if she's seen anyone?'

'No, it's all too far-fetched. It's ridiculous. Someone's trying to spook me and they've succeeded. I'm scared of my own shadow these days. I keep looking around to see if someone's following me. I've started wearing hats and sunglasses. It's a joke. But no, don't try and find anyone. I think it might have stopped now.'

'God, I hope so. But be careful. Keep your phone on you all the time. Ring me if you're worried; I'll come over to yours if ever you don't feel safe.'

'Thanks, Laura, you're the best. Let's change the subject. I don't want Ted to worry about me. Tell me about your kids. What have they been up to?'

They talked about family until Ted and Richard came back to the table with pints in each hand. The quizmaster distributed new sheets for the music round and the threatening notes were temporarily forgotten.

In the car, that evening, Laura told Richard about the notes and the word 'murderer' on Erin's front door.

'That's just crazy! And you think it could be to do with when you were in the youth club?'

'I don't know. It's the only death she's really experienced, I think. If it was me getting the notes it'd be different. I see death all the time, and people often react badly in stressful situations; an angry father who thinks I could have saved his child, maybe… I could imagine someone grief-stricken doing something like that. But Erin's a teacher, she doesn't have to deal with death every day. Then I was wondering if it could be something about a fatal traffic accident, but she's never had a road accident, even a minor one, as far as I know.'

'Hmm. What about this Malham thing? Was there more to it than meets the eye? Did you have suspicions about it? Maybe someone is blaming Erin for something someone else did?'

Laura thought hard before answering. 'Yes, there were definitely real tensions that day. Tom was furious about something, I don't know what. Fiona seemed cross too. Erin was really miserable, and Millie was – well, she was always a bit crazy. No-one was in a good mood. The weather was awful, we were wet and cold, hungry… But murder? No, impossible.'

And what about you, Laura asked herself. What was your role that day? You spent the whole time wishing someone was dead. Willing it to happen, praying for it.

What if…

Chapter Sixteen

Over a month had passed since the paint incident. Erin no longer jumped when the phone rang. She once more parked her own car in the college car park. She checked the letterbox and her pigeonhole without giving it a second thought. She had convinced herself that the episode was a random prank, a teenage dare. Ted had repainted the front door a cheerful sage green. It was a vast improvement and Erin even joked to Ted that the vandalism had done them a favour. This was true in more ways than one; she began to notice and appreciate Ted's solicitousness, his selfless support. She no longer found home life so stultifying; instead the house had become a refuge, a place of safety. She noticed tiny changes in the way they communicated with each other; the way she rested a hand on Ted's shoulder now when she leaned over his chair to ask if he wanted another cup of tea. The way he put a hand on her back when they crossed a busy road. Ted's fastidiousness, which previously used to set her teeth on edge, now felt comforting. The way he polished her shoes at the same time he did his own; the way he dried little remaining drops of water from plates with a tea towel as he emptied the dishwasher. The way he insisted on going down the aisles in the same order at the supermarket, instead of zigzagging from one thing to the next as she wanted. All this used to drive her mad, used to make her rail against his lack of spontaneity, but now she wondered why it had all seemed to matter so much.

The children, Beth and Matt, had come home that weekend to celebrate Ted's fifty-third birthday. Ted hadn't wanted a party, but had preferred a family get-together. They'd gone for a long, muddy walk, then eaten at the Indian restaurant with Ted's parents. The kids were enthusiastic about the puppy idea, and had helped her research breeds on the net. Ted had made a few enquiries to springer spaniel breeders. All in all, life was returning to normal. Better than normal even. Life was good.

Now Erin stood at the kitchen sink, happily replaying memories of that weekend as she handwashed some glasses. Ted's face as he opened his presents: a connected watch from herself, joke t-shirts and a malt whisky bottle from Beth and Matt. Her joy at seeing her bright, energetic kids pushing and shoving each other playfully on the walk as she strolled behind, arm in arm with Ted. She hummed along to the eighties playlist she'd put on Spotify.

It was growing dark outside. She placed the last glass on the draining board and reached for a tea towel. She started to dry the first glass, then casually reached up a finger to press the button to send down the electric blind. Then she stopped dead. The glass dropped from her hand and shattered on the tiled floor, sending needle-like splinters in every direction. She was only vaguely aware of her own reflection in the window pane; it was another sight that held all her attention.

A face stared back at her, almost at eye level, just feet away but separated by the glass. It was a woman. She looked old. Her hair was pulled back, but grey tendrils had escaped and straggled to her shoulders. Her skin was slack and puffy, the eyelids drooped and the mouth was set in a downwards curve. Her cheekbones were hollowed out, as if she was sucking in her breath. But it was the eyes that transfixed Erin. They stared back, bloodshot and completely expressionless.

And then the woman smiled. One of her front teeth was missing.

Erin screamed and jammed her finger to the remote. She

shut her eyes as the blind started to come down, horribly slowly. When she heard the final click, Erin dared to look again. Her heart was thumping in her ribcage. She ran to the other windows and closed the blinds, then checked the front door was locked. She didn't dare go outside to confront the woman. Instead she went upstairs to the back bedroom and put her face to the windowpane, trying to peer down into the garden. It was empty. She did the same in the front bedrooms, hoping to catch a glimpse of a retreating figure. Nothing. The woman had disappeared.

***

DC Evans was not much help. He'd descended the stairs of the ultra-modern police headquarters and shaken her hand, before leading her to a quiet side room and offering her a seat.

'Mrs Dankworth. How can I help you? Have you received another threatening letter?'

'No, not exactly. Someone came into my garden last night.'

'OK. And why did this concern you?'

'There was something odd about her. She was bizarre. It felt like she'd been watching me for a long time.'

'Did this woman cause any criminal damage?'

'No, nothing.'

'Did she threaten you in any way?'

'Well, yes, by being there! On my property. She scared the life out of me!'

'Did she say anything to you?'

'No.'

'What did she do?'

'She smiled.'

Erin knew this sounded ridiculous. A woman had come into her garden and smiled at her. The policeman clicked his pen on and off, then scratched his head. He looked impatient.

'Did you recognise this woman?'

'No.'

'Can you describe her in more detail, please?'

'I'd guess she was in her mid-to-late sixties maybe, grey hair, bad skin, missing teeth. She looked like she was wearing something black, but I couldn't see much of her body, just her face.'

PC Evans noted down the description. 'Did you see anything at all to connect this woman to the notes you received?'

'Well, I think it's connected, obviously. People don't just come into your garden and spook you without reason.'

'There's not an awful lot I can do I'm afraid. You say this woman was elderly. Do you think she could have been someone suffering from Alzheimer's maybe? Someone that got lost and ended up in your garden?'

'Well, I suppose it's a possibility… But I felt really scared. She looked menacing, somehow.'

'Of course you were scared, it's not every day you look through the window and there's a face looking back at you. I'm sure it was a shock. I've taken a note of everything you've said, but there's really nothing more I can do at this stage. But of course, come to the station or phone us if anything else happens.'

'But can't you…'

But PC Evans was already slotting his paper back into the file. He got up from his seat, indicating the interview was over. 'I'm sorry, we've got all the details but there's no action we can take,' he said again. 'But thank you for coming. Now, if you wouldn't mind…?' He raised a hand towards the door. 'We're very busy today, I'm afraid. There's been quite a spate of car thefts recently.'

Erin had no option but to precede the constable to the door, shake his hand and leave the building. She was annoyed with herself; she hadn't managed to convey the fear she'd felt, the certainty that this woman meant her harm. Something about that smile, the way the thin lips had opened to expose decaying teeth, the way the eyes remained completely lacking in expression. It was like something from a horror film. She shivered.

***

When Ted got home later that afternoon, he did a complete tour of the garden. He had done so the night before too, but it had been too dark to see much. This time, again, he found nothing. No footprints in the flowerbed, no object out of place.

'Let's have a think,' he said. 'There's probably a logical explanation. Are you sure it wasn't one of the neighbours?' he asked.

'Yes, of course. Definitely not.'

'And not someone selling something?'

'Don't think so. Besides, it was a bit late.'

'You sometimes get strange people going door-to-door selling household products, you know, sponges, dishcloths, that kind of stuff. I think it's something they do for ex-offenders. It's a kind of social rehabilitation scheme. They usually hold up some sort of a badge, a permit. Did she have anything like that?'

'I only saw her face.'

'Did she look like an ex-con?'

'Well, yes, I suppose she did. Definitely down on her luck. I suppose it could have been that. But why did she come to the kitchen window, not knock at the front door?'

'Maybe she knocked and you didn't answer. Did you have the radio on?'

'Well, actually, yes, I had Spotify on, come to think of it.'

'Loud?'

'Pretty loud.'

'There you go. It could have been that. An ex-offender comes to the door selling clothes pegs or whatever, rings the bell, gets no answer, comes round the side, smiles at you…'

'And I scream and pull the blind down!'

'You probably scared the shit out of her too.'

'Do you really think it could be that?'

'Honestly, I'm not sure, Erin. But it could be. Try not to worry about it. You're bound to be on edge, hyper-aware of every little thing that's odd just now. But it could well be something as simple as that. Now, let's have a glass of wine and get some food delivered. What do you fancy? Curry? Chinese?'

Erin made an effort to smile, and to put her fears behind her. She decided she would go for Ted's version of events; she didn't want to fall back into the swamp of paranoia again; that wasn't who she was.

I'm a strong, independent woman, she said to herself. I'm not going to cower in my house, I'm not going to disguise myself with hoodies and sunglasses. If someone's trying to intimidate me, they can fuck right off.

There's nothing to be scared of.

If I ever see that woman again, I'll march right up to her and ask her what the fuck she's playing at. I will *not* be intimidated!

Brave words…

Chapter Seventeen

Two more weeks passed. Erin was busy at work. The students' tourism projects were going well and the first group had organised their excursion last week: a half-day trip to the National Coal Mining Museum. Erin hadn't visited before and found the experience fascinating. She'd loved descending down the deep shaft, learning about the miners' way of life, hearing all the anecdotes. The only part she hadn't enjoyed was when their guide, an ex-miner, without warning put the lights out so they could experience the extraordinary depth of the darkness. Just for that moment, she felt a loss of control, and panic started to take hold. Her throat tightened and her breath became shallow. She realised she was sweating. She felt a mad urge to shout, to escape, to grab hold of the nearest person. But it was just for a few minutes, then the lights came on once more and she was able to smile and be the confident teacher her class expected her to be.

'Have you ever been to the mining museum?' she asked Laura now. 'I didn't realise how good it is. It's cheap too, you get a fantastic experience for your money.'

'No, never. I've always meant to go. Another one of those things that I never seem to get around to.'

They were once more walking, with Dudley the ancient dog. They'd parked in the Pugneys Country Park car park and picked up the path that ran clockwise around the lake. In the distance they could see the ruins of Sandal Castle, standing proud on its earth mound, silhouetted against the skyline. It was a simple walk, flat but rather muddy. Several families had had the same idea, and small children in wellingtons rushed up to stroke the dog with clumsy hands. Dudley stood patiently, sending doleful glances towards his owner.

'I loved it. But I had something like a panic attack when I was down there. I've never had that before. It was weird.'

'Really? There's techniques for controlling them, you know, if it happens again.'

'Are there? What do you do?'

'There's the five-four-three-two-one technique, that's good. You distract yourself by thinking of five things you can see, four things you can feel, three things you can hear, two things you can smell and one thing you can taste.'

'Hmm, well I'm not sure that would have worked. Couldn't see anything, hear anything, feel anything – but you could smell the coal. And almost taste it actually. Anyway, I'll try that if it happens again.'

'Were you thinking about that old woman in the window when it happened?'

'No, I've kind of put that out of my mind. But I suppose on a subconscious level I'm still a bit scared.'

'Yeah. Well, it's no wonder. But you haven't had any more notes or anything?'

'No, nothing.'

They reached the far side of the lake, then continued up to the castle. Not much remained of the thirteenth century building, just the broken remnants of the barbican tower and traces of a defensive wall, but the views from the top were good. The Calder valley stretched out before them, with the spires and towers of the Wakefield skyline painted blue in the far distance.

'Did you know this is supposed to be the castle the Grand Old Duke of York marched up to?' said Erin.

'What, in the nursery rhyme? With his ten thousand men?'

'So they say, yes. It's probably where the Duke of York was

killed.'

'I really don't know my local history, it's shameful,' said Laura. 'When was that?'

'In the Wars of the Roses. Fifteenth century, I think. There was a big battle down there, where those farms are. Must have been thousands of people killed.' Erin shivered. She pictured clashing broadswords, spears and pikes, horses thundering towards each other, armour glinting in the sunlight. And the end of the battle, when the ground would have been strewn with corpses and the air filled with the screams of injured horses. Why was she so prone to these gloomy thoughts lately? She gave herself a mental shake.

'It must have been an enormous castle at the time. Hard to imagine now though. People nicked the stones to build their houses.' She gave a last glance at the ruins. 'Shall we go back down?'

The path dropped once more and wound back along the far shore of the lake. They paused at the bird hide to admire the ducks and geese on the water, then went back along the muddy path for the last stretch to the car park.

'Is that someone leaning on your car?' asked Laura.

'Yeah, I think it is! Cheeky bugger!' A figure was resting against the bonnet of Erin's little red Suzuki. It was too far away to make out any details, but the person seemed to be looking in their direction. 'They'd better not have scratched it.'

They negotiated a particularly deep and squelchy patch of mud, edging around it, jumping from patch to patch of slightly raised ground. Dudley walked through the middle, oblivious, mud clinging to the long fur of his legs.

'Oh, Dudley, you idiot dog. We're going to have to try and get him into the water, he's filthy. I'm not putting him in the car like that.'

Laura hauled him down the bank by the collar and they tried, unsuccessfully, to get the dog to take a few steps into the lake by throwing sticks in. 'Oh well. I've got a towel in the boot.'

By the time they reached the car park, the figure had gone. There were a dozen cars there, but no people.

Laura suddenly stopped in her tracks, putting a restraining hand on Erin's arm. 'Erin, hold on. I think there's a note on your windscreen.'

Erin swallowed. She glanced at Laura, then back at the car. They both scanned the horizon looking for a figure, but all was quiet.

'Shit.'

'It could be nothing. An apology for bumping your car or something. Do you want me to go and see?'

'We'll both go.'

As they neared the car, Erin could see that the paper was blue. Oh no, oh no, she thought. Not again, please. Taking a deep breath she plucked the paper from under the wiper and unfolded it. She frowned.

'What's it say?'

'Look.' She handed the note to Laura.

ELM ROAD 9 PM TOMORROW

'Whoever it is wants to meet me.'

'Elm Road! It's got to be something connected to the youth club. But don't go, it could be dangerous!'

Erin squared her shoulders and blew out a long breath. 'I'm so sick of this. I just want it to be over. I've got to go. I can't live with this perpetual worry. I'm going to go, confront this old woman, whoever she is, find out what the hell this is all about.'

'Erin, no!'

Erin looked at Laura, her eyes beseeching. 'I just want it to be over,' she said again.

'Well if you must go, you've got to take Ted with you.'

'I can't. He's at that conference in Birmingham.'

'Oh shit.'

'Laura,' Erin knew that this was maybe the biggest favour she had ever asked her friend, 'will you come with me?'

'Oh God, you always drag me into stuff I don't want to do...' she complained. 'Honestly, I don't think either of us should go.'

'Please? I'll go on my own if I have to.'

Laura sighed. 'Then I guess I'll have to come with you,' she said. 'But I think Richard should be there too. Just in case things turn nasty.'

'I know I keep saying it, but you are a star. I don't deserve a friend like you. Really.' She put the note carefully in the glove compartment. 'How can I repay you?'

'You can hang on to Dudley while I get the towel,' said Laura, with a weak smile.

Erin took hold of the dog's collar as Laura walked towards her own car. This must be the end scene, she thought. The final act. I'll get my answers tomorrow. Then it will all be over...

But, as it turned out, there were a few more scenes to play.

Chapter Eighteen

They went in Richard's car; Laura thought it would be safer not to use Erin's more recognizable red Suzuki. He parked at the end of Elm Road and switched off the headlights. It was quarter to nine and the early November sky was pitch black. Streetlights illuminated little circles of the road ahead, but they could see no-one.

'Should we get out?' asked Erin.

'Let's wait till exactly nine,' said Laura. 'Maybe the person won't show up,' she added hopefully.

'Put this in your pocket,' Richard said to Laura, handing her a small torch. 'If anything looks like it's kicking off, flash the torch and I'll come running.' He'd already put a golf club on the back seat.

Laura grew increasingly nervous as they waited, but Erin was impatient. 'Fuck this,' she said, 'Let's go now. Let's get it over with.' She opened the back passenger door, and Laura reluctantly followed, her hand gripping the torch tight inside her pocket. They walked slowly up to the old school – but it barely existed. Through the gloom they could make out a mountain of rubble behind the steel fence, and beyond that, just the skeleton of the former cupola. Two excavators approached it from either side, like a pair of praying mantis, ready to strike the death blow.

'Sad isn't it?' said Erin. 'So many great memories there, and look at it now.'

'I'll be glad when it's gone, to be honest,' replied Laura. 'My memories aren't that great.'

They stood under the streetlamp, gazing at the demolition site. Laura shivered in the cold night air and pulled her coat tight around her. Suddenly they heard a voice, some way behind and to the right.

'Well, if it isn't Tweedledum and Tweedledee. Still together after all these years.'

They turned. A shadowy shape approached, walking casually from the other end of the street, hands buried deep inside the pockets of a long coat. As the figure neared the orbit of the streetlight, certain features began to emerge. It was a woman. The first thing they noticed was her hair: a mass of frizzy grey curls, forming a ghostly halo around her face. Her long dark coat flapped around her ankles as she walked, ever so slowly, towards them. Now, directly under the streetlight, they could see her face. Each feature - the eyes, the mouth, the cheeks - seemed to sag, as if made of melting candlewax.

'It's her,' whispered Erin. 'The woman in the garden.'

At last she stood in front of them, a slight smile on her haggard face.

'Who the hell are you?' demanded Erin, taking a step forward, her posture aggressive.

'Don't you recognise me?' asked the woman. She seemed amused.

They looked again. Her eyes were pale blue, or maybe grey, it was difficult to see under the drooping eyelids. She was tall, taller than both of them. But something about that hair seemed familiar, the way it sprang from her scalp in every direction, like frosty weeds in a winter meadow. Yes, there was something about that hair...

'Are you.... You can't be... Are you... Millie?'

'I call myself Emily now.'

Laura gasped in shock. The woman in front of them would have to be younger than they were, barely forty-eight years old, yet she had the face of a much older woman. Her skin was grey, washed out and dry, marked here and there with dark patches, like sores. The pale eyes were bloodshot and sunken. Wrinkles radiated around the mouth. The lips hung slackly, exposing the missing tooth. It was a frightening face, horrific even, but Laura's medical training kicked in. She recognised the signs of long-term drug abuse and felt an unexpected pang of sympathy for their former friend.

Erin experienced no such empathy. 'You sent me those notes,' she said, her voice hard. 'You came to my house. What the hell do you want?'

'I want you to pay for what you did.'

'What is it that you think I've done?'

'You killed Tara.' Millie stated this with complete certainty, as if it was an indisputable fact.

'What? I did not. That is completely ridiculous.'

'I know you did it.'

'You can't know anything of the sort, because it's not true.' Erin's voice rose in pitch.

'I saw you.'

'No. You are so mistaken. You are wrong, utterly wrong!'

'I want money, or I'm going to the police.'

Erin laughed out loud at this. 'You're fucking joking! This is completely crazy!' She jabbed a finger towards the woman. 'If you come anywhere near me or my family again, I'll fucking….'

'Calm down, Erin.' Laura could see this was getting out of hand. 'Let's talk calmly. Millie, why do you think Erin killed Tara?'

'I saw her,' the woman repeated.

'Are you sure? I don't think you can have,' said Laura, quietly. 'You were standing a way back from the cliff when the fog rolled in. We both were. We couldn't really see anything.'

'I know she did it. I know it.'

'Millie…' began Laura again.

'My name's Emily!' the woman snapped.

'Sorry, sorry. Emily.' Laura took a breath. 'You were a bit out of it that day, weren't you? You had taken drugs, I think. I'm not sure you were in your right mind…'

'I know what I saw.'

'OK, but if that's the case, why didn't you say anything at the time?'

'I only realised later. Much later.'

'It doesn't really hold together, Emily. I'm sorry, but…'

'You would stick up for your friend, of course. Like you always did,' spat the woman, glaring at Laura. 'Always taking her side, whatever she did. Poor you, she's still got you fooled. Don't you realise what Erin is capable of?'

'Look, I've been friends with Erin for over forty years. I think I know her pretty well. And she is not capable of murder.'

The woman snorted with derision. 'And what about you?' she asked. 'You hated Tara didn't you? You couldn't stand her. I bet you were glad when she died.'

Laura paled. 'Yes, I hated her,' she admitted, her voice barely a whisper. 'Yes, I wished she was dead. And yes, I've felt guilty about that for years. But it doesn't change the facts. I didn't kill her. Erin didn't kill her. It was an accident.' She took a step towards the woman and held out a hand, placating. 'Emily, I think you need help. I think you're still taking drugs. I'm a nurse. I can maybe get you onto a rehab programme. Let me help you.'

'Fuck off Laura, I don't need your help.' She turned again to Erin. 'I want twenty thousand pounds. I'll give you exactly one week. Bring it here, same time. If you don't get me the money, I'm going to the police. I'll tell them everything.'

'What? What exactly will you tell them?' Erin scoffed. 'That you think you saw something thirty-odd years ago when you were fourteen, and you've just remembered? Are they going to believe you? Look at you! You don't exactly look like a reliable witness. You're a mess!'

'Shh, Erin, don't be...' began Laura, but Erin didn't listen.

'The verdict was accidental death and that's exactly what it was.' Her voice became glacial, controlled. 'Accidental. An accident. Get that into your head. Now, if you continue to harass me, if you send another note, if you come near my house, if I so much as see you again, it's me who'll go to the police. I've already been twice to make complaints. There's a file on you. They've already got your little blue papers. I will accuse you of attempted blackmail. Laura will back me up. And you will probably go to prison. Who do you think the police will believe? You, with your wild accusation based on nothing at all? Or me with concrete evidence?' She glared at the woman, her nostrils flared and her breathing fast. Her words hung in the air for long seconds. 'Now, I think we're done here.' She turned on her heel. 'Come on, Laura, let's go!'

Erin stalked back to the car, her back rigid and her head held high, but Laura lingered an instant longer. As she stared at the woman, her face seemed to crumple. All the energy, the hatred and the menace had vanished, and she was once more a shabby, beaten-down figure, hunched under the streetlight. Laura searched for the right thing to say, something that would strike the right note of sympathy combined with deep disapproval. She could think of nothing. Wordlessly, she turned and followed Erin back to the car.

'I'm not sure you played that right,' she said, getting into the front seat. 'You antagonised her. She's obviously sick. She's probably got mental health issues as well as a drug problem.'

'I don't really care. She's made my life hell for the last couple of months. You can't appease someone like that, you have to come down hard. I just want her gone.'

'What happened?' asked Richard. 'Who was she?'

'Let's drop Erin off home first,' said Laura, 'then I'll tell you everything.'

Chapter Nineteen

'Tell me everything again, slowly. Start from the beginning.'

When she'd heard Ted's key in the lock on Monday evening, Erin had rushed to the door and thrown her arms around him.

'God, am I glad to see you!' she'd sighed.

'Well… um… great. I'm glad to see you too,' said Ted, letting go of his wheelie case and returning her hug.

'I met her, the woman, she was one of the old group and she tried to blackmail me and…' Erin's words were coming faster and faster, falling over each other in her haste to tell the story.

'Hold on, slow down,' said Ted. 'Let me take my coat off.' He shrugged his arms out of his jacket and hung it over the back of a chair. Next came his shoes. He lined them up beside the front door and looked around for his slippers. Erin rocked from foot to foot, impatient. Frustration started to bubble up again at Ted's fastidiousness. He put the wheelie case by the staircase and turned to her.

'Now,' he said at last, 'tell me everything again, slowly.' He led her to the sofa and they sat one at each end, facing each other. 'Start from the beginning.'

'OK. The beginning. It starts when we were young. One of the girls we knew at the youth club was called Millie. She was two years younger than us, just fourteen, and I always thought she might be bipolar. She was very excitable, a bit manic. Sometimes she seemed to be sad for no reason. Anyway, last Friday I went for a walk with Laura, and when we got back to the cars there was a note on mine, another blue note, asking me to meet someone at the old school on Elm Road. That's where the youth club meetings used to be held. Laura said she'd come with me...'

'You went? You and Laura? Erin, that was risky. You should have rung me. I'd have driven back, I'd have come with you.'

'I thought I could manage on my own. Besides, Richard came too. He sat in the car with a golf club between his knees. Anyway, it was Millie. She was the old woman in the garden – except she's not old at all, she's younger than me. She just looks really wasted. She seemed like a druggie. Anyway, she made this bizarre accusation; she said I'd killed Tara, the girl who fell off the cliff at Malham.'

'Jesus! Did she say why she thought that?'

'She kept saying 'I saw you' – but it's nonsense. Besides, even if I had done it, she couldn't have seen anything, she was standing way back and it was really foggy. No, I think she'd been hallucinating, or maybe she had, like, a psychotic episode or something... Laura thinks she's definitely got some mental health problems. So, she said she wanted money or she'd go to the police.'

'She tried to blackmail you?'

'Yes. But I just laughed. I mean, it's completely ridiculous. I told her to never come near me again, or *I'd* go to the police.'

'Then what happened?'

'Nothing. We went back to the car and drove off. And nothing since then.'

'OK.' Ted rubbed his chin, thoughtfully. 'Do you think she could be dangerous?'

'Um... No, not really. No, I don't. She was just trying her luck. She looked pretty desperate. Down at heel. She probably needed money for drugs and thought I'd be easy to scare, a soft touch, and I'd give her some money to keep her from pestering me.'

'And did *you* ever think someone could have killed this girl,

Tara?'

'No! Not for a minute. The conditions were awful that day. We were all dead scared we'd fall, especially coming down those steps from the top. It was slippery and foggy and – and I actually think it's pretty lucky no-one else died, to be honest.'

'So what's this woman Millie's full name.'

'Emily. Emily Smith. Why?'

'I don't like the sound of her. I thought I'd try and find out more about her. But Smith is such a common name. It'll be difficult. Maybe social services could help? You don't know where she lives or anything?'

'No. Probably some squat somewhere. She uses blue paper. That's the only thing I know about her, really.'

'What about the old days? Where did she live then? Did she ever talk about brothers and sisters?'

'I seem to remember she was an only child. I don't know where she lived. Wakefield somewhere.'

'Hmm. Blue paper…It's old-fashioned, isn't it? My mum still uses a blue writing block for personal letters. That doesn't help us much.'

'Wait a minute! When you said 'mum' that reminded me. I think I've got her mother's phone number somewhere. I think I remember Simon, he was another one of the old gang, writing it in an email. Let me check.'

Erin got her phone out and scrolled through dozens of emails until she at last found the one Simon had sent all those weeks before. She had completely forgotten about it.

'Here it is. Brenda Smith, Wakefield seven eight nine, two seven seven.'

'Great. That's a start.' He reached for a pen and an old envelope on the side table. 'Tell me that number again, can you?' Erin repeated it and watched Ted note it down in his careful hand. 'I might make a couple of enquiries,' he said. 'See what I can find out. It's best to know what we're dealing with, just in case.'

'Thanks Ted. You've been really good about all this.'

'That's because I love you. I might be a bit of a boring old fart, but I do love you.'

'I know. And I love you too.' She leant forward to kiss him on the nose. 'Now, tell me about the conference. Was it awful?'

***

Erin went to bed that night completely reassured. Ted's arms enclosed her, keeping her warm. The regular rise and fall of his breathing soothed her. She didn't even mind that he had chosen to wear his old-fashioned blue and white button-up pyjamas to bed, the ones that reminded her of her father and that she'd always found an instant passion-killer. No, he was her rock and he would keep the family safe. They were a team of two, and nothing bad could happen now.

That's what she thought…

Chapter Twenty

'So the Yorkshire Sculpture Park was created in nineteen seventy-seven. It was the first one in Britain, and is still the largest one in Europe today. It is situated in the grounds of Bretton Hall, which used to be a stately home, and then a further education college.'

Erin sat half-way down the coach with her clipboard in her hand. She made brief notes on the marking scheme she'd created. Voice: a little too fast. Content: good, informative. Organisation: excellent. Transport: on budget.

'The hall's closed now, but the plan is to redevelop it into a hotel in the future. The park has got some permanent sculptures, but also has lots of temporary exhibitions that change all the time. Its most famous sculptures are by Henry Moore and Barbara Hepworth.'

The student passed the microphone to her classmate, who took up the introduction.

'Most of the sculptures have been donated by the artists, or are on loan. The idea of the park is that ordinary people come and see sculpture, because most people wouldn't bother to go to a museum to see it. And it's just a really nice setting, with loads of trees, green hills and a lake. You can just come here with the kids, or walk your dog, and you see the sculptures. You don't have to try and understand them, or anything.'

Spot on, thought Erin. That's it exactly!

The third student took the microphone. 'Some statistics now. The park employs about one hundred and seventy people, and gets about four hundred thousand visitors every year. We think it could do better than that with more marketing...'

Erin lost concentration for a moment, as her phone buzzed to signal an incoming text. She took it out of her pocket and glanced quickly at the screen. A message from Ted: *Phone when you get the chance, have some info on Emily Smith.* She replaced the phone and clicked her pen on once more, as the coach drove on through the rolling hillsides towards Bretton. She didn't want to think about Millie Smith. She'd call him back later.

The coach slowed down as it passed the pretty stone cottages of West Bretton, then turned down the lane towards the entrance to the park, and into the car park. Erin was impressed that this group of four students had negotiated free parking and free entry for the whole class, arguing that it would provide good word-of-mouth advertising in the future. Also, instead of just letting the students roam at will, the group now handed round an activity sheet; ten sculptures which everyone had to try and tick off the list before returning to the coach in two hours' time. Another plus point for creativity, thought Erin, happily. She watched the students head off in pairs and small groups, papers in hand. Great, she thought. I have some free time to myself. She had always loved the sculpture park and felt completely at home there. Her parents had been on the organising committee since it first opened, and the family had visited more times than she could count. Some of the sculptures were shocking: Damien Hurst's ten-metre tall sculpture of a pregnant woman, for example, with the skin peeled away to expose ropes of muscle and a little curled foetus. The face was horrific, with its bald eyeball and grinning teeth. Other sculptures were fun and child-friendly, like the giant multicoloured octopus or the ridiculously scaled-up ice cream cone. Some were challenging – trying to make out the human shapes in a Hepworth was always a mystery to her; she preferred the gentle, burnished curves of the Henry Moores. Several sculptures blended in so well into the landscape you were not sure if they were sculptures at all, but rather the boulders, walls and ruins left over from a former age.

She wandered down the grassy slope towards the lake, admiring the tall, spreading trees, the Canada geese that strolled along the banks, and stopping now and again to check out the new exhibits. Sitting on the plinth of one sculpture, she pulled up her collar against the cold wind, and got out her phone to call Ted back.

'Hi Ted. I've got some time to myself. The students are wandering all over the park. I expect half of them will get lost and we'll have to chase them up later. But for now, it's lovely. A bit chilly, but really bright and sunny. What news have you got, then?'

'Well, actually, quite a lot. I managed to get through to this Brenda Smith woman at last. I said I was an old friend of Millie's from the youth club days, and wanted to know if she was still around. It turned out Mrs Smith was dying to talk to someone. I could hardly stop her. It's not a great story. Are you ready for this?'

'Yes, fire away.'

'Well, she dropped out of school in A-level year. I think she was kicked out for having weed in her locker, or something like that. Anyway, she went to London. It seems she got in with a bad crowd and started taking lots of drugs – cocaine, LSD, amphetamines... She had more and more mental problems and was eventually sectioned because she attacked her flatmate; apparently she was convinced her flatmate was an alien who was trying to control her, so she went at her with a kitchen knife. So, anyway, she's spent several years in and out of drug rehab and psychiatric units. She did come back and live with her mum for a while, and was off the drugs, but it didn't last too long. She disappeared again. Her mum hadn't seen her for over two years, until just recently; a couple of months ago she suddenly reappeared and asked for money. Her mum doesn't know where she's living now.'

'OK. None of that is really a big surprise. I think I'd guessed it would be that kind of thing. Well, the knife attack's a bit scary. But that was years ago, presumably. She must have had masses of psychotherapy, maybe got better?'

'Well, maybe. We don't know, but I think this might be important: I asked if she knew what Millie's condition was called, and what it meant, and this was interesting. She's got chronic drug-induced psychotic disorder.'

'That's quite a mouthful. OK, so what does it mean?'

'It means that the drug abuse has led to prolonged psychotic episodes, where she hears voices that aren't real, sees people who aren't there, believes in things that aren't true, for example. Apparently with that condition you can believe something that's obviously false, and people can show you all the proof in the world that it's false, but you won't ever change your mind. So, if she's convinced you killed that girl, nothing you say will make her see any different.'

'OK, I see. I told her again and again I didn't do it. So I won't have changed her mind, then?'

'No, I don't think so. Also your behaviour alters with this disorder. You don't have much self-control, and if you're faced with a problem, you tend to take action rather than thinking things through. So, all-in-all, I think it means she could still be dangerous. She still thinks you're a killer, and she will react by taking action.'

'Shit, now you're scaring me. Can we do anything?'

'Not much, I don't think. But keep your eyes open. Stay with people. Keep your phone on you all the time.'

'OK. I will. Thanks Ted, thanks for doing all that.'

'You're welcome. Now, enjoy your day at the Sculpture Park and forget all about it.'

'I will. It's a beautiful bright day and it just feels heavenly to be here. I'll see you tonight.'

'See you later. Bye.'

Erin stood up, brushed a few dead leaves from her trousers and set off to the right, following the lake shore, then veering uphill. The land rose gently ahead of her. The manicured lawns gradually gave way to rough pastureland as the hall and its landscaped gardens fell away. No more trees here, just a bare hillside. Groups of sheep scattered before her. This was her favourite part of the park; the wilder, more natural part. She waved to a group of students, clustered round a massive Henry Moore.

'How many have you got so far?' she called.

'Six. We can't find the weird rabbit thing.'

'I think it's back near the hall, near the big greenhouse with camellias. Good luck!'

Erin walked a little further to her very favourite spot. It wasn't a sculpture at all, more of an experience: the Deer Shelter Skyspace. Two short dry stone walls either side of a path guided the visitor towards an elegant eighteenth century structure, which was partly built into the hillside. The three graceful stone arches opened onto a space where the deer would once have sheltered from the worst of the winter weather, back in the days when every stately home worth its salt had a deer park. Behind this space, a doorway led still further into a kind of hidden chamber, buried underground. It was a stark space, pure and clean, and strikingly modern in comparison to the outside. The walls were of the palest concrete, and a continuous concrete bench lined all four sides of the chamber, inviting one to sit and contemplate. Because the focal point was magnificent: a large, square aperture was cut into the roof, through which one could gaze at the single patch of sky, marvelling at the passing clouds and the changing colours. Erin sat for several minutes, gazing upwards, letting her thoughts drift away, concentrating on nothing but the beauty of the sky and imagining shapes in the clouds. Gradually a feeling of immense tranquillity descended. She closed her eyes for a moment, as her old Pilates teacher used to encourage at the end of each class, to just enjoy the consciousness of her body, the sensation of her ribcage rising and falling with each breath, the cold of the concrete beneath her bottom. Erin could have stayed for much longer. But gradually a niggling worry that she should maybe be getting back to the hall and rounding up the students made her open her eyes.

All sense of tranquillity vanished in an instant. Sitting opposite, staring at her fixedly, was Millie. And in her lap, held quite casually, was a gun.

Erin felt her heartbeat racing and knew she was on the verge of a panic attack. She fought to keep calm. Five things, Laura had said. Five things you can see. Fuck, just concrete. Sunlight. And her. What can you hear? Nothing. Smell – only the tang of my own fear sweat. Shit, shit, shit. You stupid idiot! Why did you come in here? Stupid, stupid girl!

They stared at each other, eyes locked. In her peripheral vision, Erin was aware that the woman's coat was made of dark tweed, long and ragged at the hem and elbows. She could see the sickly pallor of her face, broken by brownish sores. But it was her eyes that held all Erin's attention. How can this be the same Millie, she thought. The Millie she once knew had wide apart, wide-open blue eyes, the eyes of youthful innocence. The woman opposite her had eyes so sunken into her head that it was impossible to determine the colour. Expressionless eyes, dead eyes, like those of a shark. Eyes that frightened Erin much more than the gun in her lap. She fought to control her breathing until, little by little, she was able to speak. Her voice was a croak.

'Is that real?' she asked, inclining her head towards the gun.

'Of course.'

'Where did you get it?' Erin had never seen a gun before. Could it be a fake?

Millie's lips curled into a smirk. 'I've got some interesting friends.'

'What are you going to do with it?'

'Shoot you, of course.'

Once again, Erin forced herself to stay calm.

'Millie, I did not kill Tara. Please believe me!'

'You did. I know you did.'

'But why do you think that? You didn't see me, did you? You lied about that.'

'She told me.'

'Who told you?'

'Tara.'

'I don't understand. Tara's dead. How could she tell you?'

Millie smiled, a kind of rictus that made her look quite, quite mad. 'She talks to me. She visits me often. She comes to my room at night. She tells me things. She told me it was you that pushed her off the cliff.'

'Listen, Millie...' She broke off as she saw the woman's face darken. 'Sorry, sorry, I mean Emily. I understand that you've had some mental health problems in the past. I'm really sorry about that. I know that part of what you've had to put up with is hallucinations. You say you see Tara in your bedroom. Don't you think that could be a hallucination?'

'I'm perfectly sane,' she snapped. 'It's Tara. She visits me. She has come back from the grave to get her revenge. She has chosen me as the instrument of that revenge.' She lifted the gun and pointed it in Erin's direction, and Erin struggled once again to subdue the panic that threatened to overwhelm her. She had to placate her, to somehow get through to her. She tried another tack.

'OK, so let's say you're right and it's not hallucinations. Let's say ghost-Tara is real. Isn't it possible that *she* made a mistake? There were six of us near the edge of the cliff that day when the fog rolled in. There was...' She counted on her fingers, trying to remember how they had all ended up sitting on the edge of the abyss. 'The first was Karen, then came Tara, then Hamza, Tom, then me, and Fiona came last. I wasn't even sitting near Tara, I was the other side of Tom. How could I have pushed her? Someone would have seen me. And why? I had absolutely no reason to kill her. She was my friend. It was an accident.'

'You weren't her friend,' Millie sneered. 'She just toyed with you. I was her friend. It's me she chose.'

Something clicked in Erin's brain. She realised that this woman was consumed with jealousy; a jealously that had begun all those years ago, and had grown more toxic with each passing decade. She had to try and build some empathy, to stay in the conversation. She needed to talk her down from the edge, like a police negotiator in a hostage situation. How did you do that? She tried to remember from the cop film she'd seen recently on Netflix. Try to appear interested. Find common ground. Build positive emotions. 'Yes, you were. You were great friends,' she said, attempting to inject warmth into her voice. 'You were always together.'

Just then, they heard voices. Footsteps sounded outside. Two people stood in the entrance to the chamber. Keira and Ben, two of the students in her class. Erin gasped, caught between relief that help might come, and an intense fear that two young people in her charge were stumbling blindly into danger.

'*Get out! Now!*' screamed Millie.

The students glanced from one woman to the other, confused, startled. Erin silently mouthed 'Help!', but they had turned away and left once more through the doorway. There was silence. Erin tried desperately to work out if they had seen the gun. Would they have noticed it, from that angle by the doorway? It was once more held slackly in Millie's hand, resting on her lap, and would have been partly hidden by her arm. Had they seen it? Would they raise the alarm? Phone the police? Or would they just wander away, thinking that the strange woman talking to their teacher had been very rude? There was a slim chance though. She had to keep Millie talking.

'Tara was your great friend,' she said, again. 'You had lots in common, didn't you? You were both only children, I think?'

'She was special. You made me sick, you lot. The rest of you, Fiona, Laura, Karen... You all treated me as an inferior, like your little mascot, or something. You patronised me, you laughed at me. Tara was the only one who treated me like an equal.'

'I'm sorry if we patronised you. I suppose a two-year age gap felt like a lot back then. We were just trying to be kind.'

'Bullshit. You enjoyed having someone to look down on, didn't you? I was a joke to you; it was obvious from the way you all looked at me. You never cared. But then Tara came and she spoke to me like an adult, she included me. She was like the sister I wish I'd had.'

Erin took a risk with her next question. It could create a breakthrough, make Millie see things differently, but it could also go horribly wrong and stoke her anger further. 'Tara was great, I know. She had some wonderful qualities. But everyone has good and bad in them. Maybe she wasn't perfect. She introduced you to drugs too, didn't she? When you were too young to handle it. Don't you think she's the reason you…' How could she put it without causing offence? 'you ended up having some problems with substance abuse?'

Millie's dead-fish eyes flashed with sudden anger. 'Substance abuse. Hah! What are you, my fucking therapist? Yes, I'm a drug addict. But that's nothing to do with Tara. No, that's entirely your fault.'

'My fault? How is it my fault?' Erin reeled from this new line of attack.

'You killed my best friend, my soulmate, my sister. Is it any wonder I used anything I could get my hands on to make me forget? You killed Tara. It's your fault I'm an addict and it will be your fault if the drugs kill me.'

'I'm so sorry you've had a difficult life.' Erin was getting desperate. Nothing she said was having the desired impact. If anything, she was making the situation worse. Millie's voice was sharp and she could see that the gun was now gripped tightly in her hand, turning her bony knuckles white. *Oh God, oh God, what can I say?*

'Can I help you? Help you get treatment? Pay for a rehab place for you?'

'Huh,' Millie spat. 'Don't try and pretend you give a crap. You're not a bleeding heart like Laura. You don't give a flying fuck. Say your prayers because you're going to die.' She raised the gun once more.

'Wait! Wait! You asked for money before. Twenty thousand pounds. I can get that for you. I could get you more. If you shoot me you'll get nothing.'

'It's too late for that. I don't want your money any more. I want blood. She demands blood.' The gun was now aimed at Erin's head.

This is it, this is it, thought Erin. This is how it's going to end. I don't want to go like this! I want my life back! I want Ted! I want to see my children again, I want to see what they do in life, who they get married to! I want to play with my grandchildren one day! She realised, all at once, that her life was amazing. It was perfect. It was precious and bright and full of sparkle. Ted was the kindest man she had ever known. She would give anything to see him again, to hold him. Why did I wait so long to realise this? I have everything! I can't lose it all, I can't! I've got to keep her talking just a bit longer.

'I didn't kill her. I wish I could make you see that. But if you're going to kill me, let it end on a good note. Tell me something, tell me your best memory of Tara. Then I'll tell you mine.'

Amazingly, the gun lowered slightly and Millie inclined her head, thinking. A little smile lifted her lips and she started to speak.

'She came to my house once. She picked me up and took me out on her motorbike. We went all the way to the coast, to Scarborough. She bought me fish and chips and we walked along the beach. I wanted to go to the amusement arcade and she gave me some money for the slot machines.' She paused for a long moment, lost in her memories. Her vision had turned inwards and Erin glanced furtively towards the doorway, wondering if she could make a dash for it. Ten seconds passed, thirty, one minute. Erin tensed, ready to run, but the woman snapped her head back towards her and started talking again. 'I won a little pink rabbit. I've still got it. It's the only thing I own that means anything to me. The only physical thing left that connects me to her. Then we went under the pier and smoked some weed. We laughed so much that day. It rained on the way back. We got soaked. Mum was so mad.'

'That sounds wonderful. She was kind to you. So my favourite memory...' She couldn't tell Millie about her own motorbike trip; that would further inflame her jealousy. Instead she thought back to the first time she saw Tara. 'It's that first night she came to the group. The way everyone stopped talking and just stared at her. She was so different; she had this aura. I remember her purple Doc Martens and her black nail polish. I was so impressed....'

'Enough now.' Once more the gun was raised. 'I'm not interested in your stories. It's time.'

'Wait, wait!' begged Erin. 'Don't shoot me! I didn't kill her. You can't shoot me!'

Millie looked around, as if noticing her surroundings for the first time. She took in the pristine beauty of the chamber. The gently sloping walls looked grey in the shadows but changed to the colour of pale honey in the sunlight. She looked up at the skylight, now free of cloud and impossibly blue. She nodded her head, slowly.

'No, maybe not, maybe not...'

Erin slumped back against the wall, relief flooding though her. She let out the breath she had been holding.

'No, I can't shoot you here. I don't want to splatter your brains all over these clean walls. Although... huh... some might call that art. No, we'll go into the woods.' She stood up. 'You go first. Walk normally. If you run I'll shoot you in the back. Stand up now!'

What do I do, thought Erin. Should I stay here? She said she won't shoot me here. Am I safer here? But if I go outside it could buy more time. There might be someone there. Maybe someone will see us.

'Hurry!'

Erin tried to stand. Her legs wobbled and she stumbled, putting a hand on the bench to steady herself.

'Get up! Go to the doorway and walk through.' Millie followed close behind as Erin approached the entrance. The gun was in her voluminous coat pocket and she prodded it into Erin's back to force her forwards. 'Move!' she commanded.

Outside the chamber, Erin's eyes darted quickly right and left, hoping against hope that there would be people to signal to. She saw no-one. Only a group of sheep, who stared at her with complete disinterest, their jaws working mechanically. She felt a jab in her back as Millie pushed her further down the hill, towards a thick clump of winter-bare trees. Erin walked as slowly as she dared, each second of life precious. But inevitably they reached the first few trees. Brambles and ferns grew between them, forming a low barrier. She stopped. This was disastrous. No-one would see them once they entered.

'Go in further!' Another jab in her back forced her to step forward.

Erin pushed through the undergrowth. The brambles caught at her trousers and snagged her boots. She looked about wildly, seeking a means of escape. Could she pick up that dead branch and swing it behind her? Could she pretend to stumble and kick the gun out of Millie's hand? Let a low branch swing back into her face? Again the gun prodded against her back, and Erin knew that it was useless. There were no more options. She was empty. Drained. A kind of weary acceptance started to replace the frantic helter-skelter of her thoughts. This is the end. Nothing more to fight for or worry about. It would all be over soon.

They reached the centre of the clump of trees. 'Stop here,' commanded Millie. 'Kneel down.'

Erin did as she was told. The gun was now level with her head. She stared down the black barrel, waiting for the moment of death. Just get on with it. I can't do this any more. Just do it. But Millie was taking her time.

'Tara!' she called. 'Tara, come to us now. This is the moment of your revenge. Come and watch me do it.'

There was silence. No birdsong, no movement, nothing but a deep, heavy silence. They waited, a frozen tableau under the dark trees. Then a little rustle, as a gust of wind shook the tops of the trees. A cluster of greying leaves spiralled lazily to the ground. Erin shivered. *The dead are all around us*, she remembered Tara saying. *They communicate with us.* She could almost believe it. Could almost imagine catching a glimpse of a ghostly figure gliding between the trees, long hair floating, green eyes flashing in a pale face. More gentle rustling, a little louder this time, and the sound of a distant twig snapping.

'She's here!' Millie smiled beatifically, a kind of ecstasy lighting up her heavy features. 'She's here!' She lifted the gun parallel to her shoulder, her arm straight, her finger tightening on the trigger. Erin closed her eyes. She waited.

It all happened so fast. She heard a noise, a dry click, then a grunt of pain. Had the gun misfired? Erin dared to open her eyes. Millie was standing in front of her, her head thrown back and her spine arched. Her arms were splayed out to the side and the gun dangled loosely from her stiff forefinger. She seemed paralysed, immobile. Then, from either side, two shapes converged upon her, taking an arm each and quickly lowering her face-down to the ground. Police. One of them had what looked like a yellow and blue Nerf gun in his hand. It looked faintly ridiculous, like a child's toy in his meaty adult hand. Erin resisted a mad urge to giggle. They kicked Millie's gun away, leaned over the prone figure and removed something from her back, then handcuffed her. Erin remained on her knees, staring vacantly as one of the policemen stepped towards her and squatted down by her side.

'Are you hurt?' he asked. Erin just stared at him blankly, uncomprehending, still kneeling stiffly on the damp ground.

'What's your name, love?' asked the other policeman, joining them.

'Erin,' she managed, before the tension left her body and she sank to the ground.

'Are you hurt?'

'N...no, I'm OK.'

The two policemen lifted her gently to her feet. The shorter man put an arm around her waist and led her slowly out of the trees, while the taller man stayed with the prone figure on the ground and unclipped his radio to call for back-up.

Two young people hovered anxiously on the edge of the clump of trees. Erin's muddled brain finally made a connection: Keira and Ben, her students. Her precious, her wonderful students. She stumbled towards them.

'Was it you? Did you call the police?'

Before they could answer, she broke down into violent, racking sobs, her whole body shaking. The policeman supported her, speaking calming words, as the two students looked on in awkward embarrassment. Erin pushed the policeman aside, bent almost double and vomited onto the grass at her feet. Then, still shaking, she straightened up and wiped her mouth on her sleeve. Keira smiled at her, a little nervously, and Erin attempted a smile back.

'You've 'ad a miraculous escape, luv,' said the policeman. His thick Yorkshire accent and deep voice had a wonderful calming effect. 'You're very lucky. These two kids 'ere were very brave. They phoned the station and then 'ad the foresight to hide behind that building there and keep watch.' He pointed to the Deer Shelter. 'The emergency call came through while we wuh driving up the M1 – that were right lucky again; we wuh just near junction thirty-eight. They'd never 'ave got 'ere in time from Wakefield. And we'd both done our taser training course, as well. Not everyone gets to do that. So, all in all, it's been your lucky day, I'd say. You should put a quid or two on the lottery tonight.' He chuckled kindly.

Erin could hardly take in a word.

'Come on, then, can you walk a bit? We'll all move down to the patrol car, if you're OK, and sort everything out back at the station. OK?'

Suddenly, Erin had a thought: 'What about my students? I have a whole class of students in the park. I can't just leave them!'

'Don't you worry about that, luv, we'll tek care of it. There'll be a whole team on its way here shortly.'

'OK,' said Erin, meekly. The policeman linked his arm through hers and the four of them slowly made their way down the grassy slope towards the rough track where the police car stood waiting.

'Wait,' said Erin, as the policeman opened the car door and stood aside for her to get in. 'Can I phone my husband? Can he meet us at the station?'

'Go on then, luv.'

Erin pulled out her phone. Her fingers were still trembling and she took several attempts to unlock the security pattern. She keyed in the number and waited, praying 'pick up, please pick up!'

'Hello,' came his voice, reassuring and warm.

'Hi Ted.' Erin's voice came out too high and she paused, trying to sound more normal. 'Can you get away from work and meet me at the police station?'

'What's happened? Are you OK?'

'I'm fine. I'm absolutely fine. I'll explain everything when I see you.'

'You sure?'

'Yes, I'm fine.'

'OK, I'm on my way.'

Erin cut the call. She realised that all she wanted to do was fling her arms around her husband and bury her face in his chest, feel his reassuring bulk, his protective arms around her. Tears rolled down her cheeks again as she got into the car. Keira sat beside her and shyly handed her a tissue. Ben sat in the front seat, looking at the dashboard instruments with interest, excited to be a part of the whole adventure.

'What will happen to the woman, Millie?' Erin asked.

'She'll be tekken t'hospital first for a medical examination. Then we'll see. We'll do a ballistics check on the gun, see if it's real and loaded. She'll most probably be charged with attempted murder.'

'She's mentally ill. She's got a psychotic disorder.'

'Then I reckon she'll likely get treatment rather than a prison sentence. Don't worry about any of that now, you just concentrate on yersel'.'

Erin leant back against the car seat and closed her eyes.

It was over.

Chapter Twenty-one

Erin had been off work for two weeks. She was a wreck. She slept badly, thrashing about in the bed, waking suddenly in a cold sweat. Her concentration was shot. She was unable to make the simplest decision: what to eat for breakfast, whether to phone the children again, what to wear. She stayed inside the house, unwilling to face the outdoors. Ted crept out of bed in the morning, leaving her sleeping. He worked a short day, then got home early each afternoon to finish his work remotely. He never once criticized her for spending the whole day sitting on the sofa watching mindless television programmes or scrolling through social media. He set about making the dinner without complaint and tried to distract her with amusing stories he'd found in the papers.

Laura came and sat with her when she came off an early shift, and on her days off. She often brought Dudley, and Erin found that stroking the old dog, looking down at the whorls in his fur, unpicking the tangles in his silky ears, made it easier to talk. The repetitive motion of her hand somehow made it possible to focus her scattered thoughts into a more cohesive order so that she could begin to process what had happened. She found she wanted to talk through the events of that day again and again, as if going through every detail could desensitise her to their impact. Laura listened, never showing impatience.

'I nearly died! I was literally just seconds away.'

'I know. Is it like they say? Did your life flash before your eyes?'

'No, I felt sort of calm. It was weird. Sort of relieved that I didn't have to think about anything any more, I could just let go.'

'I think that's probably normal. How do you feel now?'

'Shaky. All my certainties have gone. I don't trust my decisions any more, I just want Ted to take care of me. It's like my brain just fogged up.'

'Classic reaction to shock. It'll get better. Give it time. It sounds like it's cured your wanderlust, though. You're not yearning for adventure any more?' Laura teased gently. 'Not planning to leave Ted and go volunteering in some third-world country?'

'Oh, God no! I can't get past the fucking front door. I don't even want to go to the supermarket. I'm incapable of even making a bloody shopping list. Poor Ted's got to do everything.'

'How's he coping?'

'He's being wonderful. It's made me realise that I really love Ted. He's good for me. You were right about that.'

'Well, that's sort of a positive thing that's come out of it all, isn't it?'

'Yes, I suppose it is.'

Laura listened patiently, as Erin repeated the same words day after day. Towards the end of the second week, when she found Erin once more lying on the sofa in her pyjamas at lunchtime, her face clean of make-up, her hair greasy, and watching a mindless American pre-Christmas film, she decided to give her a little push.

'Erin, you can't go on like this forever. It's not you. You're a fighter. You've always been one for action. Millie is locked up until the trial. There's no danger any more. It was a horrible experience, but it's over. Finished. You've got to get back to normal.'

'I think I've got PTSD.'

'No you haven't. You've had a shock, but don't give into it. You should get back to work.'

'I can't face it. They'll all be talking about me.'

'Only for a while. And it's almost the end of term. Christmas break soon. If you go back now, it won't be such a big deal next term.'

'OK, I'll think about it, I promise.'

Erin knew that Laura was right. It was time. But she'd had another secret reason for delaying until now: Malham Cove. Her colleague Martin had agreed to cover her classes until she felt able to return. Everything had been arranged; she had managed a brief phone call with him, and e-mailed him her notes and marking scheme. He had assured her he'd take care of everything. He was looking forward to the Malham trip; he'd never been there before. By now it would have been done. She would not have to face the place again.

So Erin reluctantly phoned the principal and arranged to return to college the following week. Over the weekend she practised being normal. On Saturday she managed to get out of bed and dressed at the same time as Ted. She left the house that morning and walked to the shops to buy bread, refusing Ted's offer to go with her. She phoned for a hair appointment and drove there in her car in the afternoon. She made banal conversation with the stylist. She looked at herself in the mirror, with her new shorter cut and realised she could pass for normal. No-one would know that she'd survived a near-death experience. On Sunday she did the weekly food shop with Ted. It felt OK. She could do this.

On Monday morning she drove to college and parked in her normal spot. As she pushed open the door and walked to the second floor, she sensed the heads turning, the whispers, the curiosity of the students she passed on the stairs. In the staffroom, her colleagues were less obvious, but she was aware of their sympathetic glances, the way Henry leapt up to pour her a coffee. She checked her pigeon-hole, took a deep breath and walked up the final flight of stairs to her classroom.

She was a little late. The students were already clustered

around the door, chatting. As she approached down the long corridor, they broke off their conversations. Someone started to clap. Then another. Then a thunder of applause broke out around her. The students were grinning, happy to see her, and Erin felt a lump in her throat. She blinked back the tears and pushed through the throng to unlock the door. Once inside the classroom she felt instantly at home, relaxed. This was her territory. This she could do.

'Come on then, you lot, settle down. It's the last week of term and we've got some catching up to do.'

They didn't get down to business for a long while though; her class were openly curious and asked many questions, which she answered as calmly as she could.

'Why did that woman attack you?'

'She was ill. She had mental health problems. She was having hallucinations and thought I was someone else.' A little lie, but simpler than telling the whole story.

'Did Keira and Ben really save your life?'

'They certainly did. They were incredibly brave and resourceful. I'll never be able to thank them enough.' She smiled warmly at them.

'Were you scared?'

'Terrified!'

'Are you OK now?'

'Um, well, you'll probably find me a bit distracted, a bit dozy, but I'm getting better all the time.'

'Will the woman go on trial?'

'Yes, I think so.'

'Will you have to be there to give evidence?'

'Yes, probably. I'm not sure when.'

'Will Keira and Ben go to court too?'

'Um, yes, I should think they'll be called as witnesses.'

'Can we come and watch?'

'I don't think that's a good idea.'

Eventually the questions petered out, and Erin clapped her hands.

'OK. Let's make a start on the lesson. So, Raheebah, Ashley, Wendy and Ahmed, your excursion to the Sculpture Park was great. Well organised, informative. I especially liked the sculpture treasure hunt you'd made. Raheebah, you just need to slow down a little when you talk, take your time. Leave a few gaps so people can ask questions. Well done all of you for negotiating free entry. What about the rest of you, what did you think of the trip? Any comments?'

'The end was the best bit, when all the police cars turned up.' The class laughed.

'OK, so how did last week's trip to Malham go? Salim, were you happy with it?' She looked across at the handsome boy, a good student, intelligent. You weren't supposed to have favourites, but he was definitely one of hers. She bet he'd done a great job with his group.

'We didn't do it. We swapped with the other group.'

'What? Why?' Erin's heart sank. Oh shit, oh shit.

'We weren't ready. Amy was off sick so we couldn't get organised in time, so we asked Mr. Johnson if we could swap with the other group.'

'Oh, I see. So it's Malham this week, is it?'

'Yes, on Thursday. The coach is booked and we're all ready.'

Erin gripped the edge of her desk. She felt her heartbeat pounding in her ears. She struggled to breathe. Five things. Five things you can see. She looked at her desk: pen, marker pen, file, board rubber... four things you can feel: the edge of the table, rough and damaged. Some chewing gum stuck underneath. What can you hear? Traffic outside. A teacher talking in the next-door classroom. Smell? That distinctive classroom smell, a kind of dusty, papery odour. The pause went on for several minutes as Erin fought to regain control. The students waited, expectantly, then began to fidget and look at each other, their eyes questioning. Finally Erin looked up.

'Sorry about that. I get little flashbacks sometimes. You'll have to forgive me.' She smiled brightly and the students visibly relaxed. 'Right. Malham on Thursday then. OK. So, tell me all about the seaside trip last week. Susan, can you talk me through that, please?'

As Susan began to speak, Erin nodded along, but she was barely listening. Once more she saw the enormous limestone cliff rising up from the valley floor like a medieval walled fortress. Once more the deep crevices which cut the pavement into uneven squares, the lonely tree which fought for life on the barren rock. There was no way out of this. She had blocked it out for so long. Now she would have to face her nightmares head-on.

Chapter Twenty-two

It was over an hour's coach journey to Malham. This left ample time for the four students who had organised the trip to keep the group entertained. Erin had to admit that they were doing a fine job so far.

'The village of Malham is what they call a 'honeypot' tourist attraction; that means people come from a long way away to see it, and it's a really small place.' Salim's voice was confident, assured. He was speaking without notes, and Erin was tempted to give him top marks. 'About one hundred thousand people visit every year and the population of the village is just two hundred and thirty, so the tourists vastly outnumber the residents. Since it featured in a Harry Potter film, and since Malham was voted third best walk in the whole of the UK, the numbers have exploded. About a quarter of the buildings in Malham have a tourist function; they're hotels, bed and breakfasts, hostels, restaurants, souvenir shops, cafes, et cetera, which doesn't leave much room for normal village shops. The house prices are very high, so the young people can't afford to buy there. People in the village are divided; some are making a good living from the tourists, but others are frustrated and angry. Now I'll hand over to Amy to talk about the different problems created by tourism.' There was a bit of a fumble as Amy dropped the microphone. Feedback screeched and the listening students cringed and covered their ears.

'Sorry about that,' said Amy, adjusting the volume button. 'Can you hear me OK? Right. Well, there are lots of problems created by mass tourism in Malham. Firstly, and most obviously, parking. The car park soon gets full, and the overflow carpark in a field can't be used in wet weather. So people park anywhere; on yellow lines, blocking driveways, at the side of narrow roads. Sometimes it's so bad that emergency vehicles can't get through. Second, people don't stay on the footpaths. They wander off and cause damage to the fields, leave gates open, they drop litter which can damage the wildlife. Often people bring dogs, and they can disturb the sheep at lambing time. And there are rare peregrine falcons nesting on the cliffs. They can get disturbed if there are too many climbers. There are lots of problems to solve. Now Julie is going to talk about solutions.'

The microphone was handed over this time without incident. 'So, Malham Cove is an area of outstanding natural beauty, and people should be able to see it, but we have to manage tourism so that the beauty is not destroyed. How do we do this? One way would be to get people to use their cars less. At the moment, almost ninety percent of visitors come by private car. If people used public transport, or if there was a park-and-ride outside the village, this would help. Next, we think some parts of the cliff and the pavement should be roped off to protect the birds and the flowers there. And finally, you've got to try and educate the tourists, but in a nice way. To get them to stay on the footpaths and keep their dogs on leads. A lot of people do their research on the internet before coming to Malham, so maybe there should be more advice on the website about how to behave. We talked to Mr. Price at the Yorkshire Dales National Park Authority, and he said...'

Erin's attention began to wander. She stared out of the window as the coach left the industrial outskirts of West Yorkshire behind and started the steady climb into the Dales. Modern red-brick housing estates gave way to long, low stone-built terraces which clung to either side of the road, their stonework blackened by centuries of coal fires. After a few miles these gave way in turn to scattered farmhouses, pretty villages and winter-green pastureland. The trees were skeletal. A scattering of snow dusted the tops of the fells. The sky was overcast and threatened rain.

All too soon, they reached the village of Malham. It was a picture-perfect Yorkshire village, tiny, but full of character, with pretty stone cottages, a small village green, a couple of friendly pubs, stepping stones over a river and a beautiful, small arched bridge. Despite the grey winter weather, it was a cheerful sight. Erin began to wonder why she had dreaded coming here so much. The coach pulled into the car park and came to a stop. On a chilly winter Thursday the car park was almost empty, and it was hard to imagine it packed with hordes of summer visitors.

Salim took the microphone again, before the coach opened its door to release them.

'OK, looking at the weather, I think we should start with the walk to Malham Cove, then picnic at the foot of the cove. We'll all be walking at different speeds, so there's no point trying to stick together, so shall we say meet at the base of the cove at one o'clock for lunch? Then in the afternoon we'll visit the village. We'd like you all to try and find some locals to interview about how tourism affects their lives. We've made up a questionnaire which we'll give out after lunch.'

As the students began to get up from their seats, Erin quickly made her way to the front of the coach and took the microphone. 'Thanks, Salim. Just a word of warning before you all head off,' she began. 'If you go up to the top of the cove, it can be slippery and dangerous. Please don't go near the edge. It's treacherous and I don't want to lose any of you today!'

The door opened with a hiss and the students grabbed their bags and coats and left the coach, eager to be outside. Erin was not at all sure they'd taken her warning seriously. She took a moment to thank the driver, then followed the stragglers in the class through the village and north along the quiet road.

After about four hundred metres, they reached the start of the footpath. The first memory assailed her; here was the gate where they had waited nervously, while Karen, Hamza and Tom ran back to the cliff to search. She pushed the thought away. Once through the gate, the path led gently down to a little bridge over the beck, then flattened out into an easy half-mile stroll to the base of the cliff. Erin walked slowly, each footstep dragging her back to a place she didn't want to go to. She had the feeling she was being forced to relive that awful day but in reverse order, as if playing the video in her head, but on rewind. At the bottom of the giant cliff she could hardly bear to look up.

'Wow, it's amazing!' said Keira, coming to stand next to her.

Erin finally glanced up. It did look spectacular, but also pretty, picture-postcard perfect. A shaft of sunlight broke through the clouds, lighting up the rock face. She noticed the distinct layers in the greyish white rock. Incredible to think that each one was made up of the remains of millions of ancient sea creatures. In her memory the place had become nightmarish, dark and glowering, but today it was unthreatening. A group of bird-watchers angled their binoculars up to the cliff-face. A Labrador drank from the beck. An elderly couple strolled hand in hand to see the little slit in the rock where the water emerged from its cave.

'Are you coming up to the top with us, miss?' Keira interrupted her reverie.

'Oh, I'm not sure. It's a bit steep for my old legs.'

'Go on, miss, I'm sure you can do it.'

Erin was torn; she would much, much rather stay at the bottom. She didn't want to face the steps again, and even less the vast limestone pavement, but she also knew her students; they were young and reckless. At that age you were immune to danger. Some would surely be tempted to get close to the edge. She was in loco parentis – it was her responsibility to keep an eye on them. She shrugged helplessly and followed Keira to the start of the four hundred steep, narrow steps that led to the top of the cove. She kept her eyes down, her mind as blank as possible, concentrating on each step. It was much easier this time; still a tough climb, but the stones were thankfully dry. Had she really found this so dangerous before? When she reached the top she gasped. The limestone pavement was exactly as she remembered it. Huge and barren and quite magnificent in its otherworldliness. The lone tree was still there, twisted and bare, its branches silhouetted against the blue-grey sky. Her legs were trembling from the climb. Giving Keira a shaky smile, she picked a path over the cracks to the far side of the pavement, as far from the edge as it was possible to go. Here she sat, getting her breath back. She watched her students as they hopped from stone to stone, taking selfies and shouting to each other. They looked so happy, so carefree. This didn't have to be an evil place, she realised; it could be a giant playground, fun, exciting. Her breathing slowed. Maybe coming here was a way to drive out the ghosts of the past. Maybe this was just what she needed, in fact. She could do this. Just a few more minutes and they could all head back down. Just a few more minutes, then she'd never need to come here again. New memories would have taken the place of the old, superseding, erasing the bad ones. Almost done, almost... Her thoughts were interrupted by a shout.

'Miss! Miss! Ashley's dropped her iPhone down the crack!'

Oh God, no! A group of six students were standing a couple of paces from the edge, peering down into one of the crevices. For a minute, Erin's memory played tricks on her and she saw a different group of young people, sitting just a few metres further back, feet dangling over the edge.

She blinked the memory away, groaned and stood up, forcing herself to walk deliberately to where the students were standing. She peered down the crack but could see nothing. It was narrow and dark.

'Can someone ring the phone, then we'll figure out how far down it's gone,' she suggested.

A ringtone sounded and a faint light could just be seen, way down.

'Oh dear. I think you've had it, love,' said Erin. 'I'm sorry. Was it a good phone?'

'Yes, I just got it for my birthday. My parents will kill me!'

'That's really tough luck.' She felt sorry for the poor girl, who had tears in her eyes. 'Hold on tight to your phones, the rest of you. We don't want any more getting lost.'

Erin glanced beyond the heads of the students and suddenly realised just how close to the edge they were. Her vision became blurred, her head began to spin and she felt the churn of nausea rising in her throat. Her legs threatened to give way and she sat down suddenly.

'Are you alright, miss?'

'Oof! Yes, I'm fine. Just a bit dizzy. I'm just going to sit here for a bit.'

'Put your head between your knees.' The students crowded round her, concerned.

'I'm fine, really, I'll be OK in a sec. Don't bother about me, you go on exploring. I'll join you in a minute.'

'Shouldn't we stay with you for a bit?'

'No, no, I'm fine.' She waved them away.

One by one, the little group dispersed, leaving Erin quite alone, sitting barely two metres from the edge. Memories started to seep back. All the things she had locked away in a little box and buried deep, deep down. She had mentally cast that box to the bottom of the sea. Gone, forgotten. She had instinctively avoided it, gone round it, pushed it back down when it threatened to bob up to the surface. And now she could no longer control it; the catch had burst, the lock was broken. Images were creeping into her head like gas from a punctured waste container lying on a seabed. She could do nothing to stop them.

She once again saw the four figures sitting on the edge, their backs to her. Karen, Tara, Hamza and Tom. She saw herself nervously picking a path over to them, and Tom holding out a hand to help her sit beside him. She saw again the wonderful vista; the lush green valley below, the crows which wheeled about beneath them, the purple distant hills. She remembered the perfect stillness, as the five of them had absorbed the view in silent reverence. It was a magical moment; the five of them suspended in awe, experiencing the same thing in the same way at the identical moment. Erin had felt almost painfully overwhelmed with love for these people, for nature, for Yorkshire. She wished she could freeze this feeling of joy, of belonging, of perfect bliss. Then she remembered hearing Fiona's voice, strident, annoyed, begging them to get up, warning that the weather had changed. She felt again the fingers of mist closing around them, becoming thicker and thicker by the minute. The creeping dampness which clung to her hair and her clothes. Fiona shouting again, panic in her voice. They had stood up, one by one, very carefully, and inched back just a pace from the precipice. She remembered looking back, seeing no-one. Laura, Simon, Millie - all lost in the fog. She saw again that Karen was moving away, then Tom and Hamza. Then they, too, disappeared into the mist.

Just herself and Tara. They stared at each other, barely two metres apart. A breeze was lifting the ends of Tara's hair. Her green eyes seemed to have absorbed all the colour of the valley floor. She stood proud and straight. God, she was so beautiful. Magnificent and elemental. Now I can talk to her, now she'll understand, thought Erin. The incredible splendour of this place, it must have affected her, like it did me. Softened her. Erin felt full of love and hope and energy. She moved closer to Tara, close enough to see the minute individual raindrops that had settled on her blonde eyelashes. She would make things right.

'Tara, I love you. You're my inspiration, my idol,' she began.

Tara remained motionless, a statue.

'You've made such a difference to my life. You made me come alive! I was caught off-guard last night and I'm sorry. Can we start again? Can we get back to where we were? I love you.'

Erin reached out a hand to touch a strand of Tara's hair, as the hill fog swirled about them. It felt, to Erin, an impossibly romantic moment, alone together, isolated by the mist, frozen in time. Like a scene from a movie. She smiled, her heart full.

Tara gripped the hand that was touching her hair. Her grip tightened. 'You're nothing, Erin.' Her eyes had turned the colour of slate. Her voice was completely emotionless. 'You're a boring little schoolgirl. You lead a conventional life with your conventional family in your conventional house. You're not special. You'll have a dull life. You won't travel. You'll get an uninteresting job. You'll marry an uninteresting man and have two uninteresting children. You are Miss Average in every possible way. I've been wasting my time on you. You're nothing to me!'

Erin had turned to stone. She gaped, open-mouthed. This wasn't possible! Rejection was not possible. She couldn't just be dropped like this! She snatched her hand back. Anger started to well up, replacing all other emotions. It blinded her just as much as the tears that filled her eyes.

Then Tara laughed. She threw back her head and laughed.

Erin could no longer bear it. She turned away, her back to Tara. Then paused.

'Go on, run away, little girl. Run back to your boring little friend Laura.' Tara's voice was right in her ear, so close, so spiteful.

And that's when it happened. Without even looking, Erin reached one hand behind her. The hand made contact with a damp rain jacket. She pushed, once, hard. Her hand met resistance, then nothing. There was no sound. No scream. Nothing.

Erin turned, looked. The space where Tara had been was empty, save for the swirling mist. Tara was gone.

I didn't do that, she thought. I didn't just do that. No, no way. That wasn't me. Nope. Nope. Not me. Erin began to construct the box that would bury her action forever.

She turned and made her way carefully to the steps. She made out the shapes of Simon, then Laura. Without a word she took her place on the stone stairway, concentrating on each step, her mind totally focused.

By the time she had reached the last of the four hundred steps, she had almost convinced herself.

I did nothing. Nothing at all.

Coming back to the present with a jolt, Erin pondered. Had she done the right thing to keep silent? What else could she have done? If she'd told the truth she would have ended up in a young offender institution. Her parents would have been devastated, broken. Her sister Cathy would have suffered taunts and insults. What good would it have done to admit her guilt? Tara was dead, nothing could change that. It didn't really matter *how*, did it? So Erin had lied. She had lied easily, fluently. She'd lied first to her friends, waiting at the gate with them, chewing her fingernails and glancing hopefully down the path. She had lied to the police, saying 'the hill fog came down so quickly and we all moved away from the edge. I thought she was either in front of me or behind me. No, I didn't see or hear anything.' She'd lied in the mortuary, summoning tears. It hadn't been difficult to feign shock when she saw the broken body lying on the mortuary table. She'd lied again at the inquest. Each time she lied it became a little easier. Each time she found her own version of events taking on more solidity, and the sordid truth fading and blurring. By the time of the funeral she was calm and dignified. She managed to say a few words of comfort to Tara's mother outside the crematorium. She accepted the sympathy of her parents, of Laura, of school friends, as if it was her due. She became the stoic survivor of a tragic story. She never went back to the youth club again. Instead she put her head down, worked hard, got good A-levels and moved on with her life.

And now? What should she do now? Should she confess to Ted and to Laura? Would that make her feel better? Or should she find another little box to stuff these memories back into, to lock up tight and to throw far, far out to sea?

Slowly, Erin got up and walked towards the steps. She had a class to manage. Students to round up and get safely down to the valley below.

She'd think about the rest later.

Chapter Twenty-three
Five months later

It was a miserable day in early May. They had planned to walk, but the rain was coming down in sheets, ricocheting off the pavements and flattening the grasses at the side of the road. Erin drove carefully, peering ahead, the windscreen-wipers on full speed. The puppy whined and attempted to get up onto the seat from the passenger footwell. She'd already climbed through from the back. Erin took one hand from the steering wheel and tried to push her back down.

'No, Pippa, get down! Stay!'

Erin lost the battle, of course. She knew that dogs should never sit on the front seat; it was like allowing your child to sit there without a seatbelt. Dangerous for the dog and distracting for her. Possibly illegal. But Pippa had her own ideas. She looked so ridiculously pleased with herself, sitting on the front seat. Erin shrugged and fondled one silky brown ear before returning both hands to the steering wheel.

It was a relief when she finally arrived outside Laura's semi-detached house. She clipped on the dog's lead, locked the door and let herself be pulled up the path to the front door. Laura threw the door wide open and smiled.

'Come on in, quick! Isn't this weather awful!'

While Erin took off her wet coat and hung it up in the porch, Laura squatted down and made a fuss of the puppy. 'Oh, aren't you just a cutie? Who's a good girl then?' she said.

'She's not very good at all. I think we're going to get thrown out of puppy school. She just charges about like a mad thing and disrupts the other dogs.'

'She'll learn. Early days. Is she still destroying stuff?'

'Yes. We came down this morning and found she'd chewed through her new bed. Literally ripped it to pieces. Bits of fluff all over the place, and Pippa sitting there looking like butter wouldn't melt.'

'Oh dear, oh dear. I expect Dudley was just the same as a puppy. They do get better, don't despair.'

'I know I'm too soft with her. I can't bear to tell her off, and I'd never smack her.'

'Anyway, come through and we'll put the kettle on.'

Laura's house was a typical nineteen-thirties semi, with rooms leading off a central hallway. The kitchen was at the back of the house, square, slightly old-fashioned, but homely, with pine units on two sides and a small, round oak table in the middle. Pippa made a bee-line for Dudley, who tolerated her advances for a few minutes before slinking off to his basket, casting reproachful glances at Laura.

'So, how are you doing?' asked Laura. 'What's new?'

'I'm doing good. Great in fact. I know I moan about her, but getting a puppy's been brilliant for us. Ted and I walk her together, laugh about her together, clean up after her together… Ted's using his new watch to find dog-friendly walks we can do at the weekend. It's actually changed our lives.'

'That's brilliant!' Laura plonked a mug down in front of Erin and searched in the cupboard for biscuits. 'Sounds like you and Ted are back in sync again then?'

'Yep, totally. Well, he still gets on my nerves a tiny bit sometimes, but that's just normal marriage, isn't it!'

'No more itchy feet? Not planning to jet off to Cambodia? Africa?' Laura's voice was teasing.

'No, I'm just making the most of the life I've got. All that stuff that happened last year, it's brought us closer together. And do you remember your bucket list idea? We've actually started making one.'

'Yeah? What's on it?'

'Ted wants to go to Iceland, so that's our summer plan, and we're going to have a go at axe throwing.'

'Axe throwing? Whatever gave you that idea?'

'Dunno, it just seemed different and fun.'

'You're mad!'

Laura marvelled at her friend's resilience. She had been a mess for barely two weeks after the attack, unsure of herself, agoraphobic, lethargic, but then seemed to shrug off all concern and had gone back to work. She'd only seen her a handful of times in the last few months, but each time she'd seemed happier, more positive. But a little bit of Laura wondered how she'd managed to put the events behind her quite so fast. There is resilience, and then there's a kind of… insouciance, insensitivity. Her thoughts were interrupted by the sight of the puppy circling round and round on the rug by the dresser, nose to the floor.

'Hey, Erin, quick, I think Pippa… Uh-oh. Too late!'

A liquid stain was turning the beige carpet material a darker shade, and Pippa was looking up at them with eyes that were entirely free from guilt.

'Oh hell, I'm sorry. Here, I'll clean it up.'

'No, you take Pippa outside for a bit so she knows where she should have gone. I'll clean it up, don't worry.'

Laura fetched a cloth and dipped it in soapy water, then returned to the rug. When Erin came back in, she got up off her knees and poured them both a second cup of tea.

'Sorry about that,' said Erin.

'Oh, no problem. She's a bit old to still be peeing on the carpet though, isn't she?'

'Yes, probably. Do you think I should take her to the vets?'

'Well, what's your toilet training routine? What do you do when she pees in the house?'

'I just take her outside. They say you shouldn't shout at them.'

'Hmm, yes but you could scold her a bit. You don't have to shout, but if you say 'Bad dog', in the right tone of voice, she'll get the idea.'

'OK.'

'And then you really reward her when she does it outside. It's just like potty training the kids, basically, same theory.'

'Hmm, yeah, I guess.' Erin seemed to have lost interest in the puppy training conversation. She took a biscuit and looked around the kitchen.

'Where's Richard today? Is he at work?'

'No, he's got that hospital appointment today. Remember? I told you?'

'Um, remind me.'

Laura sighed. Typical Erin. She'd told her about Richard's medical worry two weeks ago, but Erin had obviously not taken it in. Maybe Richard is right, she thought, maybe our friendship really is one-way traffic. But then Erin had had a lot on her mind, she supposed.

'You remember, he had the check-up for prostate cancer and his PSA levels were a bit high. He's seeing the specialist today.' Laura kept her voice light, but she was secretly nervous. She knew what a silent killer prostate cancer could be. She wondered if she would have forgotten if it had been Erin telling her about Ted. But then, she was the nurse, not Erin. What did Erin know about the prostate?

'Really?' said Erin, 'Well, fingers crossed that everything is OK. Let me know what they say.'

'Yeah, I will.' Laura pushed her worry aside. 'Anyway, changing the subject, is there any news about the trial, dare I ask? Have they set a date yet?'

'Yes, there's good news there, too. Apparently she's decided to change her plea to guilty. So that means no trial. No need to face her in the courtroom, no need to drag it all up again. It's such a relief!'

Again Laura thought how Erin always seemed to fall on her feet, to avoid the unpleasant situations in life. Well, good for her, I suppose. But how does she do it? Who's her guardian angel?

'Do you know what'll happen to her?'

'Secure psychiatric unit, I think.'

'Poor Millie. Those places can be really grim. She hasn't had much luck in life.'

'Poor Millie my arse! She tried to kill me! As far as I'm concerned they can throw away the key.'

Laura looked at her friend across the kitchen table. There was a hint of disapproval in her expression. Look at you, she thought, sitting here in my kitchen with your nice clothes and your expensive watch and your new blonde highlights. You really have no idea how tough life can be for other people, do you?

'Don't you feel any sympathy for her?' she asked. 'She used to be our friend.'

'Nope. She chose that life.' Erin shrugged. 'I'm just happy it's all over at last. I just…'

She was interrupted by the first few bars of the Captain Pugwash theme tune; Laura's mobile, sitting on the kitchen work surface, was ringing. Laura stood up and checked it.

'Oh, it's Richard. Do you mind if I take this in the other room, just in case?'

'No, sure, go ahead.' Erin was actually a bit peeved not to be included in the news. She helped herself to another biscuit as Laura left the room, and gave half to the puppy.

After five minutes she grew restless. Was it good news, bad news? She decided to go out into the hallway, on the pretext of needing the toilet, and paused near the living room. The door was ajar, and she could hear Laura's voice fairly clearly.

'Yes. Yes, I see… Really? God, that must have been uncomfortable! … Well, that's good isn't it? … OK… So keep an eye on it… When do you need to get tested again? … Right… U-huh… Oh, nothing special. Erin's here, with Pippa.' Erin's ears pricked up on hearing her name, and she moved a bit closer to the door. 'Hm... Yes... I agree.' Laura's voice became more serious as she continued: 'I know. She's got absolutely no control....It's not right...Hmm.... She doesn't seem to have any idea of right or wrong.... Yes, I know..... She's got to learn that actions have consequences. You can't be allowed to get away with murder.'

Erin froze. Then swayed, suddenly dizzy. Her skin felt clammy and she thought she might throw up. Oh fuck, oh fuck! She knows! Oh God, she knows! How the hell? She heard Laura saying goodbye and returned to the kitchen quickly, her body shaking.

Laura walked into the kitchen and placed her phone on the table. She was about to tell Erin about Richard's good news, when she suddenly did a double-take. Erin was sitting upright in her chair, her hands clenched in her lap. All the colour had drained from her face. Her eyes were staring fixedly at Laura and her mouth turned down at the corners. She looked dreadful, as if she'd suddenly aged twenty years. Before she could ask what was wrong, Erin spoke:

'How long have you known?'

'Known what?'

'You know, don't you?'

'Sorry, what are you talking about?'

'I just want to know, have you been pretending all these years that you didn't know?'

'Erin, I'm not following here.'

'Don't deny it. I heard you talking to Richard.'

'So...?'

'I heard what you said about me.'

'I didn't say anything about you, I don't think.'

'Don't lie. I know that you know. I heard you say 'She can't get away with murder. Actions have consequences.' It's obvious that you know.'

'But I was talking about Pippa, the dog. She's got to learn that... What do you mean? What did you think I was talking about? Getting away with murder?'

Slowly realisation dawned and Laura's eyes grew wide with shock.

'Murder... You...?'

Erin realised her mistake. Her thoughts whirled as she tried to find a way out. Could she back-peddle, claim it was a joke, a misunderstanding? How could she spin this? But the damage had been done. She saw disbelief change to confusion, then disgust in Laura's face. The two women stared at one another for several long seconds.

'This is about Tara, isn't it? Did you kill her?' Laura demanded.

Erin closed her eyes briefly, but when she opened them, she was defiant. 'Yes, I did.'

'Fuck. Oh fuck. But why?'

'She pushed me to it. I thought she was my friend but then she suddenly just turned on me. She goaded me, laughed at me, called me boring and conventional.'

'But that's no reason... That's... that's... For God's sake! What did you do to her?'

'I pushed her. I don't think I even realised what I was doing. It was just a reflex. It was so quick.'

'Oh Christ! So Millie was right all along. You killed her.'

'Yes.'

Then Erin shrugged, as if to say 'what else could I do?' and Laura was suddenly furious, incandescent with rage.

'You bitch. You fucking bitch! You've taken me for a fool for all these years. Thirty odd years I've stuck up for you, I've been there for you, and you've been lying to me all this time!'

Erin had never, in all their years of friendship, seen Laura like this, and she was astounded. 'No, no, not really,' she said. 'I was too young, I couldn't face up to it...'

'Don't give me that bullshit! You could have told me at any time. You could have told me the truth when Millie turned up. Oh, you played your part well, then, didn't you? Poor Erin, being accused by a mad woman. Let's all help her. Bloody hell!'

'No, it wasn't like that, it wasn't on purpose, I'd kind of convinced myself I didn't....'

But Laura didn't want to hear excuses. 'And when Tara died, I was in bits! I went to a therapist for months, I felt awful, and you just sailed on and got your bloody As at A-level, fucking hell! Have you no shame? Did you feel no remorse?'

'Yes, of course, I...'

'And you went to the mortuary. You actually offered to go to the mortuary and identify her body. Just how ice-cold are you? Do I even know you?'

'Laura, of course you do, it's still me, I'm the same person I always was, I just made a mistake...'

'A mistake? A mistake? You are a murderer. You killed someone. Bloody hell. Does Ted know?'

Erin paled. Her hand flew to her throat. 'Oh, God, Laura, you can't tell him. Please, please, you'll ruin my life.'

'You have no idea, do you? You have no fucking idea! Richard is right. You're a self-obsessed, selfish, unfeeling bitch. I don't want to know you.'

'Laura, please! You've always been on my side. Please help me now!'

'I'm done with you.'

Erin sat, her eyes pleading, shaking her head, her hands raised in supplication. 'What are you going to do? Are you going to tell Ted? Will you go to the police?'

'I don't know. I don't know. Just go away. Leave me alone.'

'Please don't tell anyone, Laura...'

'I've got to think. Just go!'

'What can I say to make you...?'

'*Go!*' This last word was a shout.

Erin stumbled to her feet. For one crazy moment she wondered, just fleetingly, how she could shut Laura up, neutralise the threat. Laura was sitting at the table, head in her hands, eyes screwed shut. She wasn't looking. She could... Then she came to her senses. God, what were you thinking? She called Pippa and left the house, as quickly as she could.

She was not sure how she made it home. She drove on autopilot, unaware of cars or pedestrians or red lights. Somehow she made it back to her house. She poured a big glass of whisky to try and stop the shaking, and sat down. Think! Think! What can I do? But she knew there were no more cards to play.

I've lost my only real friend, she thought. I might lose my husband. My job, my home. It's in Laura's hands now. And I can do nothing about it. It's all up to Laura. Worst of all, it's my fault! It's all my fault. If I hadn't gone chasing memories of the old days, none of this would have come out.

Stupid girl, you thought you were untouchable, bulletproof, didn't you?

Well your luck just ran out.

Chapter Twenty-four

The next two weeks were torture. Erin alternated between wishing Laura would contact her, put her out of her misery, and then, moments later, dreading it. The same questions went round and round in her head. If Laura tells Ted, will he stay with me? Will he understand? She thought, on balance, that he might. But if Laura went to the police, if the whole thing came out, *then* would he stay by her side? What would the children think of her? What would her parents say? Could you go to prison for a crime committed that long ago? She would lose everything. But then, she told herself, it's just my word against Laura's. Perhaps all is not lost. There's no evidence. If I stick to my story, as I've always done, I can still get away with it. Maybe. Or if I say it was just an accident, I lost my balance, put a hand out to steady myself and accidentally pushed her? Was too scared to confess? Wouldn't that work? But she was so tired, so tired of the lies.

'You're very quiet today,' said Ted one morning over breakfast. 'You've been a bit out of sorts for a while. Is anything wrong?'

'Oh, no, not really. I'm just a bit tired. I didn't sleep too well. It's probably the thought of all the marking I've got to do. I hate exam time. ' She smiled at him across the table. Tears came into her eyes, unbidden. Poor Ted. Poor unsuspecting Ted. If only you knew what a deceitful bitch you're married to.

'I know what'll cheer you up. I've been thinking, it's a while since we did the pub quiz. Shall we phone Richard and Laura and see if we can get the team together again for Friday?'

Erin paled. 'No! Oh, no!' she croaked, horrified. She realised she'd reacted much too quickly, spoken too sharply. She replaced the piece of toast she was holding back on the plate and stared at it. What excuse could she come up with?

'Whyever not?' Ted looked mystified. 'Didn't you enjoy it last time?'

'No, it's not that...' Think, think, quick, think of something... 'It's just... um... It's just that I've had a bit of a fall-out with Laura.'

'Really? But you two never fall out! What was that about?'

'Um... she was a bit critical about Pippa. Gave me quite the lecture about dog training, actually. Pippa weed on her rug and she took it badly, said I was not doing puppy training right. We had a bit of a row.'

'Well, goodness, that's nothing to fall out about. You can sort that out in no time. Let me phone Richard and...'

'No, I really don't want to. Not yet. I'm still angry at her.'

'Well, OK, if you're sure. I'm positive it'll blow over in a day or two.' He stood up. 'Right then, better go. What have you got on today?'

'Not so much. No lessons. But I've got to attack the marking pile. Wish me luck!'

Ted put his bowl in the dishwasher, rinsed out his tea mug and came back to kiss her on the top of her head.

'You'll be fine. You always dread it, but you always do a good job.'

He fetched his coat and bag, called out a cheerful 'Bye! See you tonight.' and left for work. Erin remained seated, hating herself. Another lie, told so easily, so glibly. And dear, trusting Ted had swallowed it without a second thought. She sighed and stood up. She looked at her work bag which lay in the corner of the room, its sides bulging with exam papers. She wasn't in the mood for this, but knew she had to make a start. But not just yet... She decided to walk to the bottom of the lane and check the mail first. Then she'd make a second cup of tea, look at her emails. Then maybe put some washing on – and then she'd get down to work. She slipped her feet into her new blue Crocs and walked down the lane to the letterbox.

It was a beautiful spring day. The clematis was in bloom, a lovely delicate pink that covered the side wall and smelt wonderful. The peonies that Ted had planted in the front bed were just coming out too. Erin's spirits lifted as she admired the tulips and delphiniums in her neighbours' front gardens. She opened the letterbox and took out a small stack of letters. The usual stuff: bill, charity begging letter, flyers for a new restaurant. Then there was something different, a handwritten envelope, thin. Her heart started thumping as she recognised Laura's writing. Oh God! This is it! Now she would know what she was facing. She stood for long minutes, eyes closed, the letters in one hand, the other hand gripping the letterbox for support. When her heartbeat at last slowed, she turned and made her way back to the house. She sat once more at the kitchen table, with the envelope in front of her.

For some reason, she was reminded of the day her A-level results came through. There was no email back then, no list put up in the school corridors. The letter had dropped on the doormat and she had picked it up with trembling fingers, then sat, holding it in her hand, not daring to open it. *My whole future will be decided by this letter*, she'd thought. *Will I get into the university I most want to go to? Will I go to university at all?* And now, over thirty years later, another letter would decide her future. Everything pivoted around this moment. Taking a deep breath, she ripped it open. Laura's neat and gently sloping writing filled both sides of a single sheet. She started to read:

Erin,
To say I am disappointed in you is a massive understatement. I

am deeply shocked by what you told me. I couldn't stand Tara, it's true. I knew she could be cruel. I bore the brunt of that more than anyone. But what you did, it's indefensible. You took her life away at such a tender age. You robbed her of being a wife, of having children. You robbed a mother of her only daughter. Maybe your gesture was instinctive and unplanned, as you claim. But what you did afterwards is the worst part. You brushed it all away so easily. You lied to all of us, you played the shocked friend, you let us comfort you! And you've been lying ever since.

What I find so hard to take is your capacity for self-delusion. Your total lack of remorse. You say you were pushed to it; it wasn't your fault. You've managed to convince yourself that you didn't do anything so very bad.

Even now I expect you're playing the victim, thinking 'poor me, my life may be ruined, what am I going to do?' Have you thought, really thought for a second, about Tara? You killed her. Think what that means. Think about her! You used to idolise her, you hero-worshipped her. Think about her now. Can't you remember what she meant to you? Think hard about her, and then think that you snuffed that person out.

I don't want to ruin your life. I respect Ted too much for that. I love Beth and Matt almost like my own, and would never want to do anything to cause them unhappiness. I don't want to have to tell them. I won't go to the police. But I can't bear to let you get off scot-free, to push this latest thing under the carpet and act like nothing happened.

What I want from you is an act of contrition. I want you to prove to me that you have taken on board the gravity of what you did. That you get it! That you are really, truly sorry.

I don't know what you will do to prove that to me; it's up to you. You need to find a way to atone. Only if I believe you are sincere, will I keep your secret. But be assured – if you fob me off with some half-hearted apology, then I will tell Ted.

So it's up to you. You can buy my silence with what you decide to do now.

Let me know.
Laura

Erin read the letter over and over. The truth of Laura's words began to sink in. She hadn't really thought about Tara, not properly. She'd been far more concerned about trying to save her own skin. She'd spent the last fortnight worrying how to preserve her home, her marriage, her world. Although she had started to despise herself, and the part she had played, she'd not thought about Tara. She read the letter once more. Two phrases stuck in her head: act of contrition and atonement. She reached for her laptop and looked up a definition of contrition. The first definitions were connected with religion. It seemed to be a strong part of the Catholic faith and tied to the notion of sin; confessing your sins, detesting your sins and vowing never to sin again. In the Catholic faith it seemed to be possible to make an act of contrition with a short prayer. That would definitely not be what Laura had in mind. Another, more secular definition gave the example of carrying out community work as a kind of penance. Could she do that? Volunteer for some deserving charity? Was that enough, though? It sounded too much like self-aggrandisement – oh, look at me, aren't I a good person. No, not that. A third definition talked about repentance accompanied with a complete change of character. But was it really possible to change your character? At the age of almost fifty? Yet another talked about offenders escaping a prison sentence if they expressed contrition to the victim's family. But how could she contact Tara's mother? What could she do after all this time to make things better for her?

She typed atonement into the Google search. The first definition that popped up was religious again: *the reconciliation of God and humankind through the sacrificial death of Jesus Christ.* That didn't help at all. Wikipedia was more to the point: *Atonement (also atoning, to atone) is the concept of a person taking action to correct previous wrongdoing on their part, either through direct action to undo the consequences of that act, equivalent action to do good for others, or some other expression of feelings of remorse.* OK. So that was what she had to do. Take some form of action. It was impossible to undo what she had done, but she could take an action to help others, or to show that she was sorry.

Think about Tara, the letter had said. Think hard about her. Erin sat still for a long time. Then she reached for a pen and found a small, unused notebook in a drawer. She began to jot down little snatches of memories of Tara - what she had worn, what she had said, what they had done together. She began to doodle little sketches in the margins: a Doc Marten boot, a lock of hair, a pint of beer topped with a froth of foam. Little by little, her mental image of Tara fleshed out until she could again picture the girl, her long, messy hair, her magnetic green eyes, the way her jeans had sat loosely on her hips. What had Tara been about though, what had she loved, believed in? She had loved her grandmother. She had loved that place up on the moors. She had loved nature and its elemental forces. She was a pagan. Erin wrote 'wind, rain, earth, fire', then 'freedom, devil-may-care, follow your feelings'. She sketched trees, flowers, a raindrop, a little bird in the margins.

Over the next few days, Erin added more words and doodles to the little notebook. She found this strangely cathartic, addictive. She kept the notebook in her pocket and jotted down things that came to mind in the daytime, but most of her memories came back at night, when she was lying in bed, on the verge of sleep. She fought to fix them in her mind so she could add them to the notebook the next morning.

She thought often about the night of the campfire. Tara had come on to her, propositioned her, and she'd been too immature to handle it. Tara had been hurt, and had put up a defensive wall. I hurt her. That's why she'd been so spiteful, it was a kind of self-defence. You rejected me so I'll reject you! We could have got past that, in time. Could have been friends again so easily.

Little by little, Tara changed and developed in her mind from the vague, blurred outline of a teenage girl, to a real, multi-layered, complex character. A girl who was not all good, not all bad. A girl who had passions, but who also had her own demons, her own insecurities. Ostara, she wrote in the notebook. Tara's real name, and the goddess of spring. She remembered Tara comparing the goddess to the spring weather: peaceful and clement one minute, then stormy and cruel the next.

Tara had been so completely alive, she realised. Vital, spirited, temperamental. If she had to choose a single adjective to describe her, that was it: alive. And she had taken that from her.

A plan began to form.

She knew what she had to do.

Chapter Twenty-five

They drove in silence. Erin kept her eyes on the road, only from time to time casting furtive glances across at Laura, trying to gauge her mood. But Laura's face betrayed no emotion. She sat still in the passenger seat, staring ahead as the road undulated through rounded valleys, past stone-built villages, small patches of woodland and lush green farmland. Gradually they began to climb into the hills. Houses and farms dropped away, leaving only the dry stone walls and the odd, stunted tree. Erin pushed her little Suzuki through the gears until they reached their destination: Keighley Moor. Here the vista became an unbroken expanse of ragged, windswept grassland, with the fells glowing purple in the far distance. It was a gloomy, desolate place, but also uncompromising, raw and magnificent. Erin parked by the side of the road and they opened the doors. Immediately they were assaulted by the wind, which whipped their hair into their eyes, battered against their jackets and thrashed through the longer grasses. The sky above them was vast, teeming with rain-heavy clouds that raced across the landscape.

'Is this the place?' asked Laura, her words almost lost in the wind.

'Yes. Her favourite place.'

Laura just nodded. Erin changed into her walking boots, tied her hair back with an elastic, then took a backpack from the boot and threaded her arms through the straps. She nodded once at Laura, said 'Right then, I'm going,' and set off, plotting a route through the boggy moorland with determination.

She had picked Laura up from her house that morning. Laura had opened the door without a word, and gestured her through to the kitchen. There she had sat, arms crossed, waiting for Erin to speak.

'Here's what I've been doing,' said Erin, nervously. 'I've been thinking about Tara all the time, like you said, and writing everything down. Here, look.'

She handed over the notebook. Laura took her time. She turned the pages slowly, pausing to read snatches of text. She saw the careful drawings that Erin had made in the margins: a campfire, a coin embedded in a tree, a motorbike helmet, a single eye, coloured green. Each page was full, the writing becoming smaller and smaller as Erin had battled against the limited space. Reaching the last page, she handed the book back to Erin.

'What next?' was all she asked. And so Erin had told her what she wanted to do.

Now Erin fought her way through the tangled heather roots towards the ancient lump of rock. The gusts pummelled her. Tufts of snagged wool fluttered from thistles like little flags. Her thoughts went back to the last time she had been here, and she could half imagine the tall, lithe figure of Tara ahead of her, her hair streaming in the wind, the same wind that now stung her eyes and caused tears to fall down her cheeks. At first merely a small, dark outline against the sky, the boulder seemed to swell and expand as she approached until at last it loomed before her. It was taller than she remembered, and filled Erin with trepidation. She wondered if she would be able to complete the task she'd set herself. But then a sudden gap in the clouds released a shaft of sunlight which bathed the rock in a golden glow. Yes, I can do this! I will do this!

Erin scrambled carefully up the face of the giant rock, and

into the small, rectangular chamber, the one Tara had called the Druid's Chair, about two metres from the ground. A chain had been added, making it easier than before. Once inside the dark chamber, she was protected from the wind, but again she noticed the eerie humming noise that emanated from the narrow tunnel leading all the way to the other side of the boulder. It seemed to be singing to her, but gently. She shrugged off her backpack and unzipped it. With careful fingers, she laid out her offerings on the floor of the Druid's Chair. These were the things she had collected over the past weeks, the objects that she hoped Tara would find beautiful. The first was a single magpie feather. Erin smoothed the stiff plumes between her thumb and forefinger and watched how the colours shifted from black to iridescent green, purple and blue. The next was a slender branch of hazel, heavy with catkins. Each catkin was shaped like a lamb's tail, but when she looked close she could see that every single one was made up of hundreds of individual yellow flower heads. She laid this next to the feather. The third object was a piece of wasp nest, paper thin, as light as air, with tessellating cells of faultless symmetry. The fourth was a sea shell, a souvenir from the Northumberland weekend. It was perfect; delicate, translucent and pink, and so silky smooth to the touch. She arranged these four objects at each corner of an imagined square, and in the middle she placed a stubby white candle. She struck a match, then another, then another until eventually the flame took. She sat back on her heels. The candlelight cast a warm glow onto the sides of the chamber, illuminating the symbols scratched on the walls. In a soft voice, she began to speak:

'Tara, you believed that the spirits of the dead are all around us, that they watch us. If this is true, then maybe you are here now, in the place that you loved so much. Maybe you are watching me now. I don't know if your mum scattered your ashes here. I hope she did.' Erin paused. The candle flickered as a breeze moved through the tunnel. Taking a deep breath, she continued. 'I am here to say sorry. I am so, so sorry. I pushed you. I ended your life. It has taken me a long time to say sorry, but I truly mean it now.' Once more the candle flickered. 'I brought you these things because they remind me of you. I don't expect you to forgive me; how could you? You were my friend, and I loved you, I killed you and I'm sorry.'

There was no epiphany. The candle didn't suddenly flare up or snuff itself out. The wind continued to hum through the chamber, as before, but Erin felt a little lighter. She had still to accomplish one more task. She threaded her arms through the backpack once more and climbed out of the chamber, then walked round to the side of the boulder. From here it was possible to climb to the top, since the rock face was slightly more inclined, and deep diagonal striations provided some footholds. It was not easy. The stone was slippery, the wind fierce, and Erin took her time. Reaching the top at last, she sat down. She looked out over the landscape once more, admiring the vast sweep of moorland and the blue-grey mass of Pendle Hill in the distance to the west. The clouds building up in the east were black and pregnant with rain. She looked down into the pool of water at her feet, which stretched about eight feet across and looked almost a metre deep at one end. The water lapped against the far side as the wind stirred it. Reaching into the backpack, Erin took out one last item: a piece of driftwood, about thirty centimetres long, polished smooth by the movement of the sea and bleached white as bone by the sun. It was a beautiful, tactile piece, naturally curved very slightly at each end to form a boat shape. Erin had painted the word 'Ostara' in gold enamel paint in the dip of the curve, and added symbols either side; two upwardly pointing triangles, one of which was dissected by a horizontal line. These were the pagan symbols for air and fire. 'I am air and fire', she remembered Tara saying. 'Laura is earth and water.'

'This is for you, Tara,' she said, and launched the little driftwood boat into the water. It rocked and bobbed happily, until it reached the far side, where it knocked gently against the rock. Erin didn't know how long she sat there, staring at the little boat, mesmerised and soothed by the gently undulating water. Raindrops started to plop into the pool, causing ripples and breaking her reverie. It was time to go. Slowly she climbed back down, her body pressed to the rock face, reaching left and right for handholds and feeling down tentatively for footholds. It was a relief to step onto solid earth again. She paused once more, as the rain started to fall more heavily. 'Goodbye, Tara,' she said, and turned her back to the boulder.

By the time she reached the road, she was wet through and freezing cold. Laura jumped out of the car as she approached.

'Here, get in. You're shivering. Get in the passenger side, I'll drive us back.'

They shut the car doors against the driving rain. Laura looked at Erin. Her hair was a bedraggled mess. Her eyes were pink-rimmed, but her expression was open, peaceful.

'You were a long time,' she said.

'Yes,' Erin replied. She smiled briefly, and closed her eyes, leaning back against the headrest. Whatever happened next, whatever Laura decided, she felt a sense of release, as if a burden she had been carrying for too long was lifting slightly from her shoulders.

Laura reached for her bag from the back seat and delved inside, retrieving a big black thermos flask.

'Lucky one of us thought of bringing hot tea,' she said, and poured Erin a cup.

They sat in silence, drinking tea, as the windows steamed up and the rain battered down on the roof. After several minutes, Laura turned the key in the ignition, turned the blower on full and switched on the windscreen wipers. Little circles of misty green began to appear through the grey condensation, growing slowly wider and wider, until they could see out again. Laura placed her hand on the gear stick, ready to make a move, but Erin laid a hand over hers.

'Laura,' she asked, her voice calm and accepting, 'do you think we can ever be friends again?'

Laura paused, her eyes on the gearstick. Then she looked directly at Erin and replied:

'I think so. Give it time. But yes, I think so. One day.'

Erin nodded and leaned back in her seat. A sense of deep calm filled her. I'm going to be a better person, a better friend, a better wife, she thought. It's not too late.

Laura revved the engine slightly and released the handbrake. 'Come on', she said. 'Let's go home.'

ACKNOWLEDGEMENT

I owe so many thanks to my brilliant proofreaders, Sheila Carrodus and Chris Sykes. Typos, spelling mistakes and grammar errors have hopefully been eradicated thanks to their wonderful contribution, and they have both improved this novel immensely. Proofreading can be a hard slog, so thank you, thank you again.

Also to my early reader, Cathy Shahani, who suggested many good plot improvements and spotted a couple of inconsistencies. You have a great eye.

To all the former members of the Wakefield Youth Hostelling Association; those teenage years with you were the inspiration for this novel, although I don't remember any of you being quite so murderous, and of course, any resemblence to any person alive or dead is strictly coincidental.

And finally to my family for their support. One day my husband will read one of my novels...

Oh, and to you, reader, thank you for reading this book!

ABOUT THE AUTHOR

Kate Leonard

Kate Leonard was born and raised in Wakefield, West Yorkkshire. She studied languages at Surrey University and worked first as a tour operator, then as a language teacher. She has lived in Switzerland, Edinburgh and Manchester. She moved to France in 1996 with her husband and two children, and currently lives near Grenoble in the French Alps

BOOKS BY THIS AUTHOR

Fall Line

"Oh yes, I remember the murder game" he said. "I still play it sometimes."

When Ellie is invited by best friend Kat to join a ski party in a remote Swiss resort, her first instinct is to say no. She doesn't like Kat's new bunch of friends, especially dark, brooding boyfriend Neil.

Reluctantly she agrees and is gradually drawn into the strange, tense circle. Each night, huddled round the fire in the isolated chalet, they play the murder game, taking turns to imagine the most gruesome, twisted way to kill someone in a ski resort.

Many years later, an unexpected invitation arrives. A reunion is planned in the same remote spot. Once again Kat and Ellie find themselves thrown together with the enigmatic group.

But Kat has been keeping secrets from Ellie. What really happened on the penultimate day of the holiday all those years ago?

Tensions mount in the chalet. The weather begins to close in and the snow falls steadily. Then, one by one, the guests start to disappear.

Could one of them be carrying out the murders for real?

The Jetty

'Do you remember that old house we used to play in? The one we called the Scooby-Doo house? I think we saw a murder there!'

When Jenny's childhood friend turns up out of the blue,

claiming that they witnessed a murder when they were just ten years old, she initially dismisses it as nonsense. You wouldn't forget a thing like that!

But Claire is persuasive, and Jenny reluctantly agrees to help find out if something really did happen on that summer day in the grounds of the decaying country house.

But the more time she spends with Claire, the more uneasy she becomes. Is she obsessed, delusional? Jenny finds herself torn between a nostalgic loyalty to the girl she used to idolise, and a growing suspicion that Claire is mentally unstable.

As she gets sucked deeper and deeper into the mystery, cracks in her marriage appear and Jenny's comfortable suburban life begins to spin out of control.

But what if a murder really was committed on that long-ago day?

And by hunting the truth, could the two women find themselves instead becoming the hunted?

AFTERWORD

If you enjoyed this novel, it would be great if you could put a review, either on Amazon, or on Goodreads.

Word of mouth is everything in self-publishing.

Many thanks!

Printed in Great Britain
by Amazon